Mr. Darcy's Fault

A *Pride and Prejudice* Vagary

by Regina Jeffers

Copyright © 2015 by Regina Jeffers
Cover Design by Sarah Callaham
Interior Text Design by Sarah Callaham
All rights Reserved.

No part of this book may be used or reproduced or transmitted in any manner (electronic or mechanical, including photocopying, recording, or by any information storage and retrieval system) whatsoever without written permission from the author except in the case of brief quotation embodied in critical articles and reviews.

This is a work of fiction. Names, characters, places and incidents either are the product of the author's imagination or are used fictitiously, and any resemblance to any actual persons, living or dead, events, or locales is entirely coincidental.

Mr. Darcy's Fault

A *Pride and Prejudice* Vagary

Chapter 1

"THERE IS NOTHING FOR IT," he said with a heavy sigh. "I will gather Georgiana from London and set a course for Pemberley."

Attempting to clarify his thoughts, Darcy stood under the trees of the well-groomed grove of Rosings Woods. He spent a long night, a night in which he saw his dreams of marital happiness dissolve as quickly as the mist drifting in from the Swale. He spent the hours of darkness composing a letter of apology and of parting for Miss Elizabeth Bennet, and a few minutes prior in the new day's early hours, he placed it in her hands with a plea for the lady to read it.

Darcy sank down upon a wooden bench that his aunt placed along the carefully cleared path. Darcy doubted Lady Catherine ever walked in this part of the grove, but it was very much of his aunt's nature to maintain carefully tended lawns and enchanting pathways leading to a nature walk.

"It is my fault," he told a rabbit, which scurried into the opening. "I sorely misjudged the lady. I assumed my consequence would secure Miss Elizabeth's approval." Darcy shook his head in disbelief. "I certainly acted in a gormless fashion. I desired the woman because she did not easily succumb to the allure of my family's position, and then I knew surprise when Miss Elizabeth acted as she always does. My fault..." he groaned before burying his head in his hands.

With his eyes closed, the scene of last evening's horror replayed across his imagination.

"In vain have I struggled. It will not do. My feelings will not be repressed. You must allow me to tell you how ardently I admire and love you."

Darcy expected Miss Elizabeth's immediate agreement, but was met instead with her cold response.

"In such cases as this, it is, I believe, the established mode to express an obligation for the sentiments avowed, however unequally they may be returned. It is natural that obligation should be felt, and if I could feel gratitude, I would now thank you. But I cannot–I never desired your good opinion, and you certainly bestowed it most unwillingly. I am sorry to occasion pain to anyone. It was most unconsciously done, however, and I hope will be of short duration. The feelings which you tell me long prevented the acknowledgment of your regard can have little difficulty in overcoming it after this explanation."

A second groan escaped Darcy's lips.

"Certainly I did not show well before the lady," he whispered harshly. "I should have guarded my words. The colonel will have a sound laugh when he learns of my folly."

His cousin's words in describing Darcy's lack

of social skill to Miss Elizabeth still echoed in Darcy's memory.

"*It is because he will not give himself the trouble.*"

"Yet, even so, how could Miss Bennet be so misguided as to think I would quickly recover from my professions of love? Did she not realize my declarations honest?"

Another would never fill the hole in his gut. Emptiness always followed Darcy about, but after taking the acquaintance of Elizabeth Bennet, Darcy thought she would make him whole. Now the yearning was stronger than ever, as if his Soul reached out, only to have its hands slapped away for being imprudent.

"How do I begin again with the image of Miss Elizabeth etched upon my heart?"

With acceptance of the impossible, Darcy stood slowly before sucking in a steadying breath.

"Lady Catherine and Ann are likely to be in the morning room. Her Ladyship will not be happy to learn I mean a speedy exit from Rosings."

Returning his hat to his head, Darcy squared his shoulders. Yet, the sound of hurried footsteps had him spinning in the direction of the gate where he encountered Miss Elizabeth earlier to observe a familiar figure weaving his way in the direction of Hunsford Cottage.

"What the devil is he doing in Kent?" Darcy growled.

If Elizabeth, when Mr. Darcy gave her the letter, did not expect it to contain a renewal of his offers, she formed no expectations at all of its contents. No longer encumbered by his sudden appearance or his equally speedy exit, she could now stomp her foot in annoyance and complain under her breath, both of which brought little relief to her anxiousness.

"Dratted man! I should have thrown his letter at his too stiff back."

Yet, instinctively, Elizabeth clasped the letter to her chest.

"It is not as if the man plans to offer you his hand a second time," Elizabeth told the rising hopes she fought hard to quash. "Foolish girl," she warned her racing heart. "A man of Mr. Darcy's importance could not be made to beg for my acquiescence."

After Mr. Darcy's withdrawal last evening, the realization of what she did made inroads into Elizabeth's resolve.

"Even though the connection would benefit my dearest family, my esteemed father would never permit me to marry purely for the bond." Elizabeth sought justification for what others would perceive as a moment of pure foolhardiness. "And God knows I could never tolerate the man's control of my life. I am not cut of the same cloth as Jane: I cannot act the martyr."

Thoughts of the pain Mr. Darcy brought to her sister's door only riled Elizabeth further.

"I have no wish in denying that I did everything in my power," Mr. Darcy replied to Elizabeth's accusation with assumed tranquility, *"to separate my friend from your sister, or that I rejoice in my success. Toward him I was kinder than toward myself."*

Elizabeth looked in the direction Mr. Darcy walked: The gentleman had turned once more into the plantation.

"I should follow him, tear up this declaration of his

superiority, and throw it into his face. How would you like that, Mr. Darcy?" Elizabeth taunted the spot where she last saw the gentleman.

Although she would never admit it aloud, recovering from Mr. Darcy's proposal was not yet achieved: Since his hurried departure from Hunsford Cottage last evening, Elizabeth thought of little else. Such was the reason she begged off assisting Charlotte in the garden to indulge her need for air and exercise.

"After last evening's headache, I fear I am totally indisposed for employment," Elizabeth told her friend.

When she left upon her walk, she purposely chose the lane, which led farther from the turnpike road rather than to face the possibility of encountering Mr. Darcy in the parkland. But Elizabeth's efforts were fruitless for Mr. Darcy appeared suddenly from a grove, which edged the park. She thought to retreat, but he saw her, and Elizabeth was not of the nature to cower; therefore, she stood her ground, moving again toward the gate, which led to the groomed grounds.

"*Miss Elizabeth*," he called while she refused to acknowledge his approach with either a curtsy or verbal reply. Mr. Darcy held out the letter, which she took without thought. He said with what Elizabeth termed as haughty composure, "*I was walking in the grove some time, in the hope of meeting you. Will you do me the honor of reading that letter?*"

Elizabeth looked down at the letter held tight in her grasp.

"I suppose I should read the poisonous missive and be done with it," she grumbled.

Reluctantly she returned to the path leading

further into the woods. As she walked, Elizabeth broke the wax seal and opened the letter, two sheets of foolscap, written quite through, in a very close hand covered by an envelope, itself likewise full.

"Rosings. Eight of the clock," she read aloud the first line. Her steps slowed, but Elizabeth continued along the prescribed path. "Be not alarmed, madam, on receiving this letter by the apprehension of its containing any repetition of the sentiments, or renewal of those offers, which were last night so disgusting to you."

As I expected, she thought, *there will be no renewal of Mr. Darcy's proposal*. Elizabeth did not know whether that particular fact disappointed her or brought gladness for the finality of the man's regard.

"I write without any intention of paining you, or humbling myself, by dwelling on wishes which, for the happiness of both, cannot be too soon forgotten; and the effort which the formation and the perusal of this letter must occasion should have been spared, had not my character required it to be written and read."

Elizabeth paused suddenly to huff her indignation.

"Naturally Mr. Darcy's unbridled pride would demand the last word on the matter. Heaven forbid Mr. Darcy practiced the idea of going one's own way and letting others do likewise. I wish he were before me so I might bring the gentleman more clarity upon the subject."

With a growl of resignation, she returned to both her walk and the letter.

"You must therefore pardon," she read through tight lips, "the freedom with which I demand your attention; your feelings, I know will bestow it unwillingly, but I demand it of your justice. Demand?" she hissed.

"When did you not demand, Mr. Darcy? And do not flatter yourself to think you know my disposition!"

Despite the fact she *unwillingly* gave into her strong curiosity to read what would amount to nothing but untruths, Elizabeth was not about to give the gentleman an inch of rightness.

With anger's bile rising to her throat, she raised her eyes to the heavens, saying a quick prayer for patience. Elizabeth stood perfectly still, seeking the goodness Jane would practice in this sham, but she could not seem to bring her emotions into check. In frustration, she sat a bruising pace, knowing she could not return to the Cottage and her friend without first burning away some of her animosity toward the man. If Mr. Collins learned of Mr. Darcy's proposal, her cousin would likely drag Elizabeth by her hair to Rosings Park to apologize to Lady Catherine for having drawn the attention of Her Ladyship's nephew.

"It is very unladylike of me to think so, but I would enjoy throttling the gentleman!" Elizabeth fumed as she marched along smartly while ignoring the beauty of God's hand, which she would customarily cherish. "How is this madness ever to end? How may I face Mr. Darcy and his aunt when all I can think upon is the gentleman's umbrage? It will be a difficult fortnight before I can escape to Longbourn."

Elizabeth glanced at the pages she held tightly to her cloak.

"Should I continue with this deceit or place it in one of Mrs. Collins's fireplaces?" she mocked.

She shook the offending letter harshly. Determined to have no more to do with Mr. Darcy, with trembling fingers, Elizabeth began to refold the pages. Yet, before she could complete the task, her eyes fell upon the lines from which she last read.

Her pace slowed once more, and unwittingly, Elizabeth read, "Two offenses of a very different nature, and by no means of equal magnitude, you last night laid to my charge. The first was that, regardless of the sentiments of either, I detached Mr. Bingley from your sister."

The man possessed a way of forthright speaking, which always challenged Elizabeth's best efforts of equanimity. Never having fully subsided, her anger roared again.

"Do you mean to deny your involvement, Mr. Darcy? You bragged of your success in the matter only last evening," she huffed.

Ignoring where her steps led her, as well as the thickening of the vegetation surrounding her, Elizabeth bit out the words as she continued reading Mr. Darcy's recitation aloud:

"My second offense, that I had, in defiance of various claims, in defiance of honor and humanity, ruined the immediate prosperity and blasted the prospects of Mr. Wickham. Willfully and wantonly to threw off the companion of my youth, the acknowledged favorite of my father, who had scarcely any other dependence than on our patronage, and who was brought up to expect its exertion, would be a depravity to which the separation of two young persons whose affection could be the growth of only a few weeks, could bear no comparison. But from the severity of that blame which was last night so liberally bestowed, respecting each circumstance, I shall hope to be in the future secured, when the following account of my actions and their motives are read. If, in the explanation of them, which is due to myself, I am under the necessity of relating feelings, which may be offensive to yours, I can only say that I am sorry. The necessity must be obeyed, and further apology would be..."

"Absurd!" Elizabeth screeched as she stumbled upon a tree root, pitching forward. Before she could right her stance, a loud click announced she wandered too far from the customary path through the woods. All she could do was scream as the trap meant for a fox snapped shut about her ankle. Her half boots did not prevent the sharp claws of the leg trap from piercing her skin.

Darcy quickened his pace, but even so, by the time he reached where the lane leading to the turnpike road marched along with the parkland's paling, he lost sight of the figure. In frustration, he turned in a circle to survey the various paths leading to Hunsford Cottage, the woodlands, and the park.

"Which way did the scoundrel flee?" He ground out the words. "I thought the dastard in Meryton." But then the obvious connections arrived. "Could Mr. Wickham's presence in Kent be the reason for Miss Elizabeth's refusal?"

Darcy's mind became a red-hot haze.

"Has Miss Elizabeth renewed her interest in the gentleman?" he whispered in harsh tones. "Perhaps an elopement is afoot. Would than not be the pinnacle of irony?" A deep sigh of acceptance escaped Darcy's lips. "If the lady's heart is engaged elsewhere, you escaped a miserable marriage, Darcy."

More determined than ever to be quickly from

Rosings, Darcy crossed to the gate to return to his aunt's manor house. He knew he should make the effort to ensure the unwelcomed visitor left the area, but he could not engender the effort. He would instruct Lady Catherine's head groom to send out men to drive Darcy's long-time enemy from the estate's land.

"And if Miss Elizabeth chooses to follow Mr. Wickham, then more the pity for the Bennets."

The sound of a dog barking somewhere off to his right had Darcy's ears straining to locate the noise. Lady Catherine's games keeper used several Springer spaniels and bloodhounds to keep poachers at bay, as well as to rid the parkland of the creatures Her Ladyship deplored.

"Perhaps the hound cornered a different breed of poacher," Darcy declared with a wry twist of his lips. "As much as I hold no desire to come upon a lover's tryst, my pride demands I know the truth."

Face first, Elizabeth smacked the ground hard. With nothing upon which she could catch a handhold, she struck the earth with a resounding thud, one that drove the air from her lungs and literally, shook every bone in her body.

"Lord in Heaven," she groaned when a breath was finally possible, as she attempted to shove her body upward upon her elbows, only to collapse again from the pain shooting up her calf. She sputtered against the clump of grass and dead leaves at her lips. "What have you done, Elizabeth Bennet?" she chastised. The pain coursed through her leg, and tears formed in her eyes. Raising her head to claim her bearings, she made a second attempt to right her position, only to be held firmly in place.

"A trap," she pronounced aloud, as the blackness fogged her thinking.

In her distracted state, Elizabeth stepped into a trapper's lure, which was bad enough, but the leg trap also caught part of the bowl of her day dress, essentially locking her right side in place. She could not bend her knee, nor could she sit to remove the trap. Elizabeth laid upon her stomach in a wooded area of the estate, a place few would think to look for her; there was no means of escape unless she created one.

"It is not as if God means to send you a rescuer," Elizabeth grumbled as she fought for a lucid thought.

Even though, she realized the futility of her efforts, Elizabeth dutifully emitted several loud calls for assistance. She waited after each for an answering response, but when none came, the fear returned to her heart. Moisture ran down her temples and formed upon her upper lip. With difficulty, Elizabeth worked her right arm free of her cloak to wipe at the droplets only to come away with blood smears upon her glove.

"What else, God?" she grumbled, realizing her nose and forehead seeped blood.

With a concentrated effort, Elizabeth raised her head to look over her shoulder to the trapped ankle; again, she attempted to move her injured foot only to be met with more excruciating pain.

"I cannot simply lie here," she groaned in frustration.

However, as the blackness staked its claim upon her sensibility, Elizabeth succumbed to the need to rest her forehead upon her arm, thinking she simply required a few moments to construct an idea for escape. The calm of her surrounds lured her closer to unconsciousness, but the sound of something moving through the woods had her alert with apprehension.

When the two dogs came bounding into the path ahead of her, Elizabeth did not know whether to celebrate or know more fear. The animals stilled with a warning growl and a barring of teeth.

"Easy," she whispered. Her heartbeat hitched higher. "Is your master about?" She turned her head slowly to look for the animals' owner. The hound put his nose to the ground and began to sniff her cloak and arm. "I am not your enemy," she said in soothing tones.

And then the dog did the unthinkable. He sat beside her and lifted his voice to the trees. The spaniel joined the hound in setting up an alarm, and if the sound were not so ear piercing, Elizabeth would applaud their efforts in her behalf. Instead, she covered the ear closest to the dog with her free hand.

"This is all Mr. Darcy's fault," she added her complaint to the mayhem, as the hound took up the call once more. "Him and his dratted letter."

With a couple of miscues, Darcy followed the sound of dogs' pleas. Yes, there were two: a hound, which split the air with his long, mournful howl, and the deep, resonant 'woof' of a working dog. Periodically, Darcy paused simply to listen to the animals ring an alarm. They evidently cornered either a two-legged intruder or a four-legged one. Darcy was betting on the former, but either way, he meant to learn the truth of the racket. However, he did not chase the sound without first removing the Queen Anne pistol he carried in his jacket and then checking the

Mr. Darcy's Fault

hidden blade in his walking cane.

Prepared for action, when Darcy rounded the curve in the narrow path, he did not expect the sight, which greeted him.

"Miss Elizabeth?" Darcy stumbled to a halt when the spaniel sat low in his haunches to growl a warning against Darcy's approach.

"Easy," Darcy said without the anxiousness rushing through his veins. He glanced to where Elizabeth Bennet lay unmoving upon the ground. Instinctively, he knelt to the dog's level. "I mean the lady no harm."

Darcy permitted the animal to sniff him before he stood again. Edging closer to Elizabeth, he cautiously examined the situation. Her crumpled form brought an ache to his heart. Seeing her such reminded Darcy of the petite fragility her frame claimed; often, Elizabeth's personality made her appear larger than she was.

"Elizabeth?" Darcy knelt to whisper into her hair. "Speak to me."

Although muffled by the earth into which she spoke, Elizabeth weakly chastised him.

"I never gave you permission, Sir, to use my Christian name."

Despite the dire situation, Darcy smiled.

"That is my darling girl," he taunted.

Raising her upper body upon her elbows, Elizabeth protested his familiarity.

"I am not your 'darling girl,' Mr. Darcy. Not your *darling* anything."

Darcy thought, *Not yet*, but instead he asked, "Where are you injured?"

She turned her head stiffly to glance at him over

13

her shoulder.

"My right ankle. While reading your cursed letter, I stepped in a trapper's lure."

Her lips were tight, and there was blood caked upon her forehead and chin.

"My God, Woman!" Darcy exclaimed as he flipped Elizabeth's cloak from his way. "Why are you not caterwauling in pain?"

Darcy's fingers trembled as they lightly brushed the steel trap, while his admiration for the woman increased substantially.

"I promise I will fill several handkerchiefs with my tears once this is over," she quipped.

Elizabeth gasped, biting hard on her lip to stifle the cry of pain, when Darcy attempted to loosen her skirt tail from the mechanism.

"I apologize, Miss Elizabeth," he mumbled as he examined the situation from a different angle.

Elizabeth heaved a heavy sigh.

"I would like to say I am your champion, but I fear my patience is dwindling. You will know success in this matter, will you not, Mr. Darcy?" she asked breathlessly.

Darcy's mind filled with unbearable pressure to yank the offending lure from her sight, but he said, "Bear with me. I promise to free you."

Elizabeth returned her head to her forearm.

"I am at your disposal, Mr. Darcy," she said wearily.

Darcy suspected her supposed calm came from a bit of delirium. He wished he fetched a groom or Lady Catherine's grounds' man before he set out upon this task, but his pride told him Elizabeth Bennet refused him because she preferred Mr. Wickham. Little did he think a letter of explanation could bring her more pain.

Darcy caught the rent in the hem of her gown and gave it a mighty yank to open the tear further. Unsurprisingly, Miss Elizabeth did not protest, a sign the lady succumbed to her peril. Gently, Darcy ran his hand along her back to check her breathing. Although weak, her breaths were as if she were sleeping.

Assured, his worse fears would know another day, Darcy reached behind him to find his discarded cane lying beside the pistol upon the ground, before giving Elizabeth's shoulders a tender shake to arouse her.

"I mean to pry the trap open," he explained. "Do you possess the strength to lift your leg free of the contraption while I hold the lure open?"

Elizabeth raised her chin from the ground.

"Tell me when, Sir." For a split second, Elizabeth's body stiffened with alertness, and then she went completely limp. From beside him, the spaniel whined.

"I agree," Darcy grumbled as he crawled on all fours to check her breathing once more.

Finding her unconscious, but breathing normally, Darcy scrambled to his feet to straddle her booted ones. Stripping away his caped coat and tossing it to the ground, he edged Elizabeth's left foot from his way; anxiously, he placed the toe of one of his Hessians on the right side of the trap, loosening the tension of the mechanism as it eased from her skin. Even so, Elizabeth did not move, a fact that worried Darcy greatly. Miss Elizabeth was likely the most strong-willed woman of his acquaintance. Her resting docilely was not a good omen, in his opinion.

Slowly and carefully, Darcy wedged the cane into

the small opening. His heart told him to hurry, but his mind kept repeating the need for great care.

"Do not wreak more damage upon the woman," Darcy said aloud. "If the trap is sprung again, it will likely do irreparable harm to Miss Elizabeth's ankle."

He swallowed hard before he placed the toe box of his left boot upon the opposite side of the trap. Using his weight to lower the left side of the lever, Darcy paused only long enough to suck in a steadying breath. Squatting awkwardly over the device, Darcy reached down to capture the curve of Elizabeth's ankle in his gloved hand. He wished he could shift his weight to keep his balance, but any swift movement could release the trap again.

Patiently, he lifted Elizabeth's foot, bending her leg at the knee. There were several jab wounds in the creamy skin of her exposed calf, and her ankle appeared badly bruised and swollen. Inch by terrifying inch, Darcy lifted her foot higher. When he cleared her limb of the trap, Darcy removed his right foot, and the lever slammed against his cane. Keeping a tight grasp upon her foot, he released the left side. This time, his cane cracked and bent. Free to rest Elizabeth's foot again upon the ground, Darcy gently lowered her leg to rest upon the grassy area. Standing to look upon his work Darcy's eyes fell upon the trap. In anger, he caught the bent metal of his hidden sword and tossed the trap against the side of a nearby tree.

Clear at last, Darcy dropped to his knees beside Elizabeth.

"I have you," he chanted as he rolled Elizabeth to her back. Darcy used his handkerchief to wipe away the trickle of blood from her nose. Unconscious, Elizabeth

Mr. Darcy's Fault

did not fight him, and Darcy took a perverted pleasure in having the right to tend her.

"You shall have a black eye, my love," he observed as Darcy checked her arms and legs for any broken bones. With the release of the pressure upon Elizabeth's ankle, the puncture wounds began to bleed, and Darcy stripped off his cravat to wrap about her leg. He would like to remove her boot, but he suspected he could cause Elizabeth more injury if he did so.

Instead, Darcy loosened the fastenings of Elizabeth's cloak to toss it upon his discarded coat. He would leave both garments until later.

"Come, Love," Darcy spoke in soft tones as he lifted Elizabeth to him. Her breathing was even, which gave Darcy hope. "Like it or not, Elizabeth Bennet, after your recovery, you will be Mrs. Darcy. You are thoroughly compromised, my girl."

Darcy turned his steps toward Rosings Park. Lady Catherine would disapprove of his actions, but he would not permit his aunt to hush up his actions. One way or another, Darcy meant to have Elizabeth as his wife. Darcy assured his pride that she would learn to return his affections once Darcy had her alone at Pemberley. His ancestral estate would work its magic on Miss Elizabeth's heart, and he would have her in his bed each night.

"My wish is for you and children," Darcy whispered into Elizabeth's hair.

With tails wagging and playful yips, the dogs rushed ahead of him as Darcy wove his way along the tree-rooted path. Neither he nor the animals took note of a dark figure stepping from behind a tree. The man scooped Darcy's coat and pistol from the ground. Turning to where he hid while Darcy tended Miss Elizabeth, the interloper bent to gather the pages of the long-forgotten letter. With a smile of conniving, the man saluted Darcy's retreating form. The interloper refolded the pages and slipped them into his jacket pocket, along with the pistol, before disappearing the way he came.

Chapter 2

As Darcy carried Elizabeth toward their future, the sweat formed upon his forehead, but he did not know exhaustion. Instead, Darcy's heart discovered peace. It was not how he hoped to claim Elizabeth Bennet, but now as he sat dutifully by her bed as the laudanum drew Elizabeth deeper into sleep, regret was not among Darcy's emotions.

His appearance upon Rosings' threshold with Elizabeth Bennet in his arms created more chaos than even Darcy imagined. Thankfully, Elizabeth did not recover long enough to hear his aunt's vehement protests. Nor did she know that to allay Lady Catherine's qualms, Colonel Fitzwilliam volunteered to name Miss Elizabeth as his wife, an action, which irritated Darcy beyond reason. After Elizabeth's refusal of last evening, Darcy would not chance the lady making a choice between him and the colonel, who Miss Elizabeth appeared to prefer to Darcy.

"I appreciate your benevolence, Fitzwilliam," Darcy said with more patience than he felt, "but it was I who compromised the lady. My duty demands that I protect Miss Elizabeth's reputation." When he noted several of Her Ladyship's servants lurking in the shadows, Darcy added, "It was I who tore Miss Elizabeth's gown, who examined her limbs for broken bones, who removed her cloak, and who tied my cravat about the lady's leg to prevent more bleeding."

To Darcy's mind, it was important not to provide Lady Catherine with the means or the opportunity to hush up word of Darcy's actions.

With a maid looking on, after the surgeon's exit, Darcy claimed the chair beside Elizabeth's bed. Mr. Panwich cleaned the multiple puncture wounds circling Elizabeth's right ankle.

"I believe I rid the wounds of threads and fragments of the lady's gown," Panwich explained. "Yet, even so, you must be certain whoever is to tend Miss Elizabeth should take care to wash the lady's wounds thoroughly each day." The surgeon glanced to the sleeping Elizabeth, who reluctantly succumbed to the surgeon's ministrations. "Your lady, Mr. Darcy, has a quick tongue," the man said with a knowing smile. "I suspect Miss Elizabeth will lead you through a up tempo Scottish jig."

A faraway look of promise filled Darcy's eyes.

"I am counting upon it, Panwich." Darcy's lips twisted in a wry smile. "Did Miss Elizabeth tell you the fault of her accident rested plainly upon my shoulders?"

A glimmer of a second smile danced across the surgeon's expression.

"The lady was most eloquent upon that particular

fact, Sir."

Darcy shook the man's hand.

"I hold no doubt. Thank you for your service to my intended."

That was hours prior. Pretending to read, Darcy's mind remained upon the sleeping Elizabeth. When she woke, she would certainly not appreciate his high handedness. Even his attending her sick bed was a calculated move upon Darcy's part so Elizabeth could not refuse him a second time. True the door remained open and a maid napped in a nearby chair, but Darcy personally overseeing her care was a purposeful break in propriety, which sent Lady Catherine into a swoon.

Over the book's rim, Darcy studied Elizabeth's perfect countenance. He had at first scarcely allowed Elizabeth to be pretty; he looked at her without admiration at the ball; and when they next met, Darcy looked at her only to criticize. But no sooner had he made it clear to himself and his friends that Elizabeth possessed hardly a good feature in her face, than Darcy began to find it was rendered uncommonly intelligent by the beautiful expression of her dark eyes. To this discovery succeeded some others equally mortifying. Though Darcy detected with a critical eye more than one failure of perfect symmetry in her form, her figure had him acknowledging it to be light and pleasing; and in spite of Darcy asserting that Elizabeth's manners were not those of the fashionable world, their easy playfulness caught him by surprise. Of this Elizabeth was perfectly unaware; to her, Darcy was only the man who made himself agreeable nowhere and who did not think her handsome enough with whom to dance.

"Foolish fellow," he chastised softly. "You were lost before you had sense enough to withdrawal."

Mrs. Collins assisted Panwich in dressing Elizabeth in night clothes before insisting her friend swallow the laudanum Panwich prescribed for pain. Darcy was thankful for the lady's loyalty to Miss Elizabeth. If the surgeon required Darcy's assistance, Darcy might be tempted to touch Elizabeth. At the colonel's warning of how poorly Lady Catherine would be judged if she refused, their aunt agreed to provide Elizabeth with the barest of care. In some ways, Darcy wished he carried Elizabeth to Hunsford Cottage rather than to Rosings Park, but then Mr. Collins would refuse Darcy's participation in Elizabeth's care, and that participation was the basis of Darcy's hopes to claim Elizabeth.

Her head rested upon a thin pillow, and Elizabeth's chestnut-colored hair spread across her shoulders. The blanket was pulled up to her chest and tucked in tightly about her body, but it did little to dissuade Darcy's imagination of her lying beneath him. Looking upon her, Darcy's jaw clenched with desire. Elizabeth's head turned to the right, exposing the slender column of her neck. How often did he dream of sliding his lips down the length of it to nimble on the pulse point where her shoulder met her neck? Elizabeth's cheeks remained a bit flushed, and Darcy reached out a finger to make certain she knew no fever.

Almost from the first moment of their acquaintance the woman invaded his every thought. It was more than simply her beauty. It was the manner in which Elizabeth challenged him at every turn. Elizabeth Bennet filled Darcy's mind with dreams of a future. Exhausted from his reverence to the past, Darcy decided he deserved a present, and he prayed Elizabeth would one day desire the same. It was a gamble–this plot to claim the woman he loved; yet, there was no controlling the longing, which brought Darcy to this moment. He thought never to act so foolish. This need he held for the woman was certainly not a welcomed emotion–not characteristic of his renowned reputation for logic. Some would term his current Bedlam as a man's lust for a comely lady, but Darcy knew his feelings so much more.

"Now, you must teach the lady to trust you implicitly," Darcy whispered in hushed tones, but as quickly as he said the words aloud, a nagging doubt sprung to his mind: He prayed the woman before him had not given her heart to another. If so, those who feared him would have the pleasure of knowing how poor a gamer he truly was: This was the first time Darcy risked everything on anything but a sure hand.

"Darcy?" his cousin shook Darcy's shoulder. "You should know your bed. You will be of no service to Miss Elizabeth if you fall ill from exhaustion."

Darcy glanced about the room, now draped heavy with shadows. While she slept under the effects of laudanum, Elizabeth took to crying out for her father and for her sister Jane, and once she mumbled what sounded of Mr. Wickham's name. It hurt Darcy's pride that his name was not upon Elizabeth's lips, but Darcy swallowed his consequence and caught her hand before whispering assurances of his devotion. He told himself afterwards that the unconscious mind often dredged up unresolved issues while one slept, and even if Elizabeth spoke Mr.

Wickham's name, it could be nothing more than her reliving their argument after his proposal of last evening.

"I would prefer to stay," Darcy said as he stretched to relieve cramped muscles. He thought it prudent for his campaign to win Elizabeth if she woke to find his tending her, and innately, Darcy knew his place was at Elizabeth's side.

"I would have a word, if you please," the colonel suggested through disapproving lips.

Fitzwilliam nodded to the passageway, and Darcy stiffly followed his cousin from the room.

"Have you thought your actions through, Darcy?" the colonel spoke in hushed tones. "I am not personally lodging an objection to Miss Elizabeth, but as your cousin, it is my duty to bring to your attention the fact the lady is not of the first stare of the *ton*. Do you truly believe placing Pemberley's future in Miss Elizabeth's hands a wise decision?"

"The prospect is more prudent than making our Cousin Anne Pemberley's mistress," Darcy replied testily.

Fitzwilliam shook off Darcy's remark.

"No one, other than Lady Catherine, would consider Anne an appropriate match. That being said, how will others judge your choosing Miss Elizabeth?"

Darcy hesitated; the time for honesty arrived.

"In truth, I care not for the approval or censure of others. I spent countless hours over the past three years in consideration of the type of woman I would require for a wife. Unfortunately, among Society, I never met a woman I thought held the qualities to make me and Pemberley whole; that is, until I took the acquaintance of Miss Elizabeth. If you insist upon having the truth of my determination, please know I am acting in this matter from more than honor: Last evening, I offered Miss Elizabeth my hand."

"You hold the lady in deep regard?" his cousin asked in awkward surprise.

"I do," Darcy responded with quiet simplicity.

The colonel's lips turned upward in a tentative smile.

"Then you have my support. Whatever you require, I am your man." Darcy thought it ironic Fitzwilliam never considered the possibility Miss Elizabeth refused Darcy.

"There is one task if you will accept it: I should have asked someone to see to this earlier, but in the chaos of finding the lady a competent surgeon, the matter slipped my mind." His cousin nodded his encouragement. "I left my caped greatcoat, Miss Elizabeth's cloak, and my Queen Anne pistol at the scene of Miss Elizabeth's accident."

The colonel's eyebrow rose in curiosity.

"Why would you have the pistol in your possession?"

Darcy's eyes narrowed as his mind searched for a response Fitzwilliam would accept.

"I heard the bay of the hounds and thought I might overtake a poacher. I dropped the gun while I attended Miss Elizabeth."

Despite his cousin's assurances, a muscle jerked in Fitzwilliam's cheek, announcing a bit of uncertainty remained.

"It will soon be too dark to search for the items this evening, but I will do so upon the morning light."

Darcy did not want to flame the colonel's doubts, but he knew Elizabeth would ask of the letter.

"Miss Elizabeth also carried a letter of a personal nature. If you would retrieve it and return the missive to her, I am certain my lady would be most appreciative." Darcy would prefer to have the letter in his possession; yet, it would be all that was vulgar to reclaim it.

"A letter?" The colonel's inquisitiveness grew by the second. "From you?"

"Yes."

"Another break in propriety? Who is this new Fitzwilliam Darcy? I feel as if all I know of you is a façade."

Darcy held the colonel's studying gaze. He swallowed the disenchantment, which marked his life. He meant to shed the indecision.

"I am as I always was, Fitzwilliam; the only exception would be the presence of Miss Elizabeth in my life, which opened me to new possibilities."

Having posted Mr. Sheffield outside her door, Darcy slipped from Elizabeth's room in the early hours of the next morning in order to freshen his clothes. Darcy thought it ironic that his trusted valet practiced more propriety than did Darcy. Lady Catherine sent her housekeeper to inform Darcy that Her Ladyship would no longer permit Rosings' household servants to provide Darcy the illusion of respectability. His aunt *suggested* he *remove* his "paramour" from under Rosings' roof.

"I will ask Mrs. Collins to tend her friend while I make arrangements for Miss Elizabeth's recovery," Darcy assured Sheffield.

"I assume we will also depart Kent," his valet asked with only the slightest lift of an eyebrow.

Darcy glanced over his shoulder to Miss Elizabeth's

peaceful repose. Her disheveled appearance pleased him.

"As quickly as the lady is prepared to travel, we will depart," he said with a smile. "Keep my belongings at ready."

When he returned to Elizabeth's chambers less than an hour later, Sheffield reported restlessness returned to Elizabeth's sleep. Darcy wished he could claim an easy sense that all would be well when she awoke, but he both anticipated, as well as feared, making an explanation of how he compromised her. Adding complication to his nagging uncertainty, the colonel returned to the manor with news that Darcy's pistol, caped coat, and the letter could not be located at the scene of Miss Elizabeth's accident.

"What means this, Darcy?" Fitzwilliam demanded when he returned Elizabeth's cloak to Darcy.

Darcy regarded his cousin with remarkable self-possession.

"Likely one of Her Ladyship's tenants thought to make an extra coin or two."

"Then why not also take the lady's cloak and even the blade within the cracked cane? They also hold value. And why a letter? It is not as if Lady Catherine's tenants have a need of something few of them could read. What are you not telling me, Darcy?"

Darcy fought the flicker of regret before schooling his expression. In truth, he held no doubts if one of Her Ladyship's cottagers discovered the items, he would return them to the manor. Most certainly, the tale of his rescue of Elizabeth Bennet became common knowledge among those residing upon the estate. And if the person who took the items was not one of those who called

Rosings Park home, then it was likely George Wickham. How that scoundrel might use his "finds," only Heaven could engender a guess. Darcy knew it would be important to secure Elizabeth's agreement as quickly as possible.

"I explained, Colonel. I proposed to Miss Elizabeth, and afterwards, I returned to my quarters to write the lady a letter of an intimate nature. In it, I thought it best if I address several of the disagreements Miss Elizabeth and I had previously, especially those regarding Miss Elizabeth's familial connections and her relationship with Mr. Wickham..."

"Wickham?" the colonel snarled. "What the devil does that reprobate have to do with Miss Elizabeth?"

Darcy did not so much as twitch a muscle, which was remarkable considering the thought of Elizabeth with his once comrade brought Darcy to murderous considerations.

"Last November, Mr. Wickham joined the regiment at Meryton. As is typical for the man, the scoundrel inveigled his way into the good graces of the Bennet sisters. He took great pleasure in belying my reputation to all who would listen. From her lips, you are aware I offended Miss Elizabeth by not claiming her hand during the amusements. As such, Mr. Wickham made Miss Elizabeth his 'special friend.'"

"And you?" Cynicism sang in his cousin's tone.

"In my explanation in the letter, I attempted to allay Miss Elizabeth's confusion regarding the man." Darcy's brow wrinkled in reflection.

Fitzwilliam accused through tight lights.

"Your *explanation* mentions the situation at Ramsgate?"

"Yes."

Appalled, his cousin's fists formed balls at his side. "Some scoundrel holds proof of Georgiana's ruination? How could you be so foolish, Darcy? Have you no care for your sister's future?"

Darcy fought for patience.

"You, above all others, know I never make a decision without first considering Georgiana's well being. I chose Miss Elizabeth to wife because I witnessed her interactions with her sisters, and I considered her as an exemplary model of sisterly affection. It was a mistake to place the tale of Georgiana and Mr. Wickham into writing, but I felt, as my wife, Miss Elizabeth deserved to know the truth of her former friend."

Something more than anger flickered in the colonel's eyes.

"If Georgiana's encounter with Mr. Wickham becomes common knowledge because of your negligence, you will know my ire, Darcy. The fault for this whole fiasco lies at your feet."

"Easy," Darcy whispered as he pressed Elizabeth's shoulder into the mattress. "You were injured and should not move so quickly."

Catching him unawares, Elizabeth had bolted upright from what appeared to be a sound sleep. Her eyes fluttered opened and closed several times.

Darcy watched as Elizabeth licked her lips, the movement providing a tug of desire for him to taste them.

"Where?" Elizabeth asked with difficulty. Her eyes twitched behind closed lids.

"You are in one of the chambers at Rosings Park."

Darcy half expected her to rail at him for being in her room. The fact she did not had Darcy akilter. During the night, he prepared his arguments.

"How long?" Elizabeth's eyes remained closed.

Darcy leaned closer.

"Only eight and twenty hours since I discovered you in the woods. You do recall the trapper's lure, do you not?"

Elizabeth's eyes opened to examine his.

"I recall, Mr. Darcy." Darcy watched as clarity claimed Elizabeth's expression. She glanced to the still opened door. "Is there..." she began. "Is there any possibility someone else brought me to this place and tended my wounds?"

Elizabeth's indignation arrived, and despite his best efforts not to do so, Darcy smiled.

"I fear not, my dear."

Elizabeth gave her head a good shake to drive away the effects of the laudanum.

"Of course, you know, Mr. Darcy, I will not permit this situation to change anything." She tugged the blanket higher. "Now please act the role of gentleman and ring for a maid to assist me."

Darcy was tempted to steal a kiss, but he placed his desire aside. There would be time to win her affection once he held Elizabeth's acceptance of the fact she would be his wife.

"It is not so simple, Miss Elizabeth," he announced with a bit of amusement.

Elizabeth screwed up her face in disapproval.

"Even so, *simple* is possible. Is it not, Sir?"

Darcy reached for her hand, but then thought

better of it.

"My aunt, as you might imagine, was not happy with my actions on your behalf. As such, Lady Catherine forbids her staff to tend you."

Elizabeth's honey umber eyes darkened with frustration.

"Her Ladyship means to punish me for a situation not of my doing? I never heard of anything so preposterous. Please ask Lady Catherine to call upon me at her leisure, and I will explain I mean to release you from any duty you think to owe me."

Darcy sat straighter: He knew Elizabeth Bennet well enough to recognize her determination to deny him.

"You will explain to my aunt that I proposed prior to your accident? Alone in Mrs. Collins's parlor?" Darcy added for good measure.

"Certainly," Elizabeth declared readily. "And I declined."

"Yet, you accepted a letter from a man not your betrothed?"

Her self-assurance cracked.

"You provided me no time to consider refusal."

"You could have called me back. Could have thrown the letter away."

Darcy recognized the truth of his accusations as they skittered across her features. Elizabeth had considered both possibilities.

He added quickly to keep her off balance. "But what I had to say after so violent an encounter piqued your curiosity; did it not? You thought perhaps I renewed my offer. Had you thought to reassess your options, Miss Elizabeth?"

She flushed the most becoming shade of red.

"No! Certainly not."

Darcy offered a cool smile: Her animated denial proved Elizabeth Bennet had second thoughts regarding his proposal. It was the smallest of fissures in Elizabeth's resolve, but it was a beginning. As if someone eavesdropped on their conversation, he leaned closer.

"And there is the matter of how I had my fill of gazing upon your well-defined legs, touching them at will, the purposeful tearing of your gown, the removal of your cloak without your permission, carrying you in my arms across Rosings' parkland, and the fact I spent the night sitting in yonder chair to watch over you." Darcy gestured to the chair he drew near Elizabeth's bed.

"You did everything possible to ruin my reputation!" she accused. "You meant to force me into marrying you!"

"I meant to see to the health of a woman I hoped to claim as my wife," Darcy corrected. '

Elizabeth's eyes flashed with fury.

"No matter whether your intentions were for good or for ill, Mr. Darcy, I shall not marry you. I will not be forced into a marriage I do not desire."

A niggling bit of jealousy rushed to Darcy's lips; yet, setting Elizabeth irrefutably against him would make his task more difficult.

"Think upon my offer, Miss Elizabeth. Among certain circles I am thought to be a fine catch. I possess more than adequate income and an estate known for both its efficiency and its beauty. As my wife, you would want for nothing." Elizabeth started to interrupt, but Darcy silenced her with a touch of his finger to her lips. "Miss

Lucas will soon return to Meryton with tales of your downfall. Even if you have no care for your position in Society, think of what your refusal will do to your family. Your lack of respectability will taint the future of each of your four sisters. Their prospects will disappear without their doing so much as batting their eyes at a gentleman."

Chapter 3

A TEAR ESCAPED ELIZABETH'S EYE to cascade down her cheek.

"Even so," she whispered, "I...I prefer to return to Meryton as Elizabeth Bennet, not as Elizabeth Darcy."

Darcy stood slowly. They remained silent for several long, agonizing minutes, while he considered the loss of his hopes, and his insides twisted maddeningly into a tight knot. Only the soft tick of the mantel's clock announced the passage of time. He proposed to Elizabeth Bennet, and although Darcy's presence in her bedchamber compromised her in Society's eyes, Elizabeth refused him. How she must hate him! Or how she must love Mr. Wickham! It was a sobering reality. Darcy wished he could return to Pemberley where he might find some peace from the insanity, which surrounded his acquaintance with a woman who felt nothing but staunch censure. A tremulous ache filled his heart. He never considered himself a coward, but the thought of a quick escape to

Derbyshire, or even to the nearest public house, beckoned.

"Miss Elizabeth," Darcy said through tight lips, but he could not formulate a clear thought when he looked upon her handsome countenance. True: Elizabeth fairly ripped his heart from his chest and stomped soundly upon it. Yet, even so, Darcy could not retain ill will against her. Elizabeth's inner strength amazed him. What other woman of Darcy's acquaintance would refuse his hand? Most would be the instigator of the ruse, which brought him and Miss Elizabeth together. The woman would make some man a fabulous wife: Elizabeth Bennet would not falter even through life's darkest days. She held amplitude of spirit and faith, which placed her above all others. "Please reconsider," he said slowly. "Too many know what occurred here. I can offer you an honorable position as the Mistress of Pemberley–an exalted place in Society."

An unladylike snort announced Elizabeth's obduracy.

"I never aspired to such a position, Mr. Darcy."

"Would being my wife be such a burden?" he asked more testily than he intended. Darcy sat heavily, his hands unconsciously balling into fists as his mind searched for relief–defensively protecting his remaining pride. "I wish only to protect you, Miss Elizabeth. As a gentleman, I cannot permit humiliation to become attached to the Bennet name."

A soft tap at the open door drew Darcy to his feet. Elizabeth smiled approvingly upon Mrs. Collins, but Darcy did not appreciate the interruption. Yet, what could he do? *Perhaps,* his mind raced with possibilities, *this is a blessing. Perhaps Elizabeth simply requires time to judge the ramifications of her decision.*

"Welcome, Mrs. Collins," Darcy said with as much civility as he could muster.

Behind him, Elizabeth called joyfully to her friend.

"Charlotte, I am pleased you came." Elizabeth attempted to shove herself higher in the bed, but a grimace announced her lingering pain. Darcy fought the urge to rush to her side and offer his comfort. "If you will assist me, we may return to the Cottage."

Mrs. Collins shook her head in disagreement.

"I think not, Lizzy. This situation brought Mr. Collins to his knees, and if I am not mistaken, from what I just overhead, you hold unfinished business with Mr. Darcy."

"Et tu, Brute?" A clear accusation of betrayal rested heavy between the women.

Darcy wished to witness Mrs. Collins's confrontation with Elizabeth. He strongly suspected his future rested upon the lady's shoulders. He might even learn more of how best to proceed with the mulish Elizabeth Bennet, but Darcy offered the pair a polite bow.

"I will leave you to your private conversation, but know, Miss Elizabeth, this matter is far from naming an end."

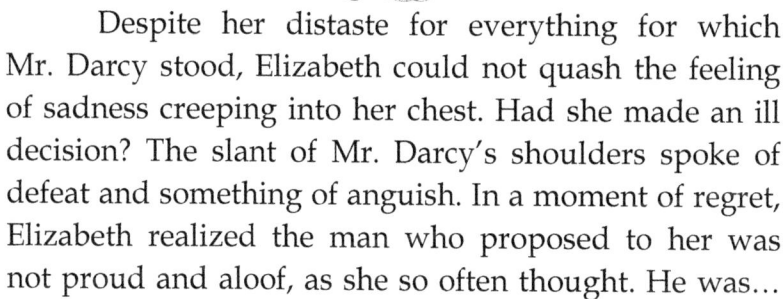

Despite her distaste for everything for which Mr. Darcy stood, Elizabeth could not quash the feeling of sadness creeping into her chest. Had she made an ill decision? The slant of Mr. Darcy's shoulders spoke of defeat and something of anguish. In a moment of regret, Elizabeth realized the man who proposed to her was not proud and aloof, as she so often thought. He was...

he was... She could not place a finger upon the words she sought. Mr. Darcy was simply alone. *Just as am I,* she thought. Their eyes met and held for what felt an eternity. She knew she should look away, but Elizabeth could not force her eyes from the gentleman's.

"I am a man of my word, Miss Elizabeth," Mr. Darcy said with purpose.

A smile turned up the corner of his lips–a genuine smile, one meant specifically for her, and Elizabeth's heart pounded wildly. Desire tore through her. *Let it be,* a small voice insisted, but Elizabeth did not want to escape the connection that claimed dominance since Mr. Darcy's profession of love. Something happened. Something changed. Something Elizabeth could not explain, even to herself. She did not understand how or when the field of play altered, she simply knew it had. With defiance, she shoved the rush of heat away.

"And I am a woman of my word, Mr. Darcy."

With her rebuke, the gentleman strode from the room.

"Dratted man! This ignominy is his fault." Mr. Darcy's exit brought Elizabeth's irrational ire to Miss Collins's door. "Why would you set yourself against me, Charlotte?"

Her friend shrugged off Elizabeth's accusation.

"Except for you, no one is set to destroy your future, Lizzy."

Despite Elizabeth's best efforts to appear unaffected, the rigorous hold on her emotions crumbled.

"What would you have me do, Charlotte? Marry a man I do not love? You of all people know my desire to join in affection–to enjoy my husband cuddling with our children–to witness his delight when I walk into the room."

Charlotte straightened the counterpane across Elizabeth's lap.

"And you cannot imagine Mr. Darcy as such? Odd. In truth, I believe the man would be quite indulgent with his wife and children. Look how he tolerated Mr. Bingley's sisters simply because he admired the man."

Elizabeth rolled her eyes in disbelief, but a secret voice said Charlotte's words smacked with possibilities. Mr. Darcy would never be accused of lighthearted recklessness, but he was intelligent and quick witted and extremely well read. Their conversations would know substance. And despite her dislike for him, Elizabeth would admit, if only to herself, the man possessed an excessively fine countenance, even when he brooded, which seemed to be quite often.

"It is my opinion Mr. Darcy holds you with highest regard, Lizzy," Charlotte continued. "I observed how he looks upon you when he thinks no one takes note. The man's eyes light with enchantment when you are moving about the room. If you could learn to show him a bit of affection, you could know great happiness."

"How do you know a bit of affection would be enough?" Elizabeth demanded. "And why is it so important to you that I reconsider Mr. Darcy's offer? I require answers, Charlotte! Speak sense to me."

Charlotte caught Elizabeth's hand before propping a hip upon the bed's edge.

"Finally, my dearest friend welcomes logic once more," Charlotte declared good-naturedly. "Lizzy, you cannot ignore yesterday's events. You were most assuredly compromised." Elizabeth longed to deny her friend's assertion, but she feared Charlotte's words held the truth. "In a bedchamber, Lizzy, and unchaperoned! Would you have your father lose his life in defending your honor?"

"Certainly not! If you must know the truth of it, the evening I declined Lady Catherine's hospitality, Mr. Darcy came to the Cottage to propose. The man is not simply acting from honor."

Her friend's eyebrow rose with inquisitiveness.

"Then I had the right of it. The gentleman holds you in affection. Please tell me you did not refuse him. Think of his connections. The Darcy name could do much for your family."

"Most certainly, I refused him," Elizabeth said in incredulity. "You should have heard him, Charlotte. He spoke as if his offer was a superior one!"

"Is it not?" Charlotte reasoned.

"Do you not recall the misery he brought to Jane and Mr. Bingley?" Elizabeth protested weakly.

"I warned you at the Netherfield Ball that Jane disguised her feelings for Bingley too well. It is likely Mr. Darcy observed what many thought to be your sister's indifference to Bingley. And in my opinion, Mr. Bingley is as much to fault as you think of Mr. Darcy. Bingley should know the stuff of his convictions."

"I explained Jane's shyness," Elizabeth countered. "And I agree with you of Mr. Bingley's lack of resolve. Yet, even if it were not so, can you imagine me as Mr. Darcy's wife? The mistress of a great estate? The woman with whom he claimed his husbandly duties?" Just saying the words brought a rush of color to Elizabeth's cheeks.

"Has the man not asked for a sign of affection?" Charlotte's tone ran rough over Elizabeth's fears. And it was Elizabeth's fear of being found wanting as Mrs. Darcy, which tightened her chest.

"Most assuredly not. I refused the man!" Elizabeth declared, although the thought of knowing Mr. Darcy's touch was not so appalling as it once was. She grimaced in a rueful manner. "Moreover, what concern is it of others if I choose to dissuade the gentleman?"

Charlotte clicked her tongue in disapproval.

"Even if you do not affect Mr. Darcy, you must think upon how your joining could benefit your family. In spite of our avoiding the subject, as longtime friends, we both realize, one day I shall be Longbourn's mistress; your family will be displaced. Mr. Darcy's wealth can protect your mother and sisters once your father meets his Maker." Charlotte tightened her hold on Elizabeth's hand. "If your reputation lies tattered, your sisters will suffer, Lizzy. No respectable man will seek them out. Jane will never welcome Mr. Bingley's return for Bingley wishes a Society connection. He could not choose a wife whose family knew scandal."

Elizabeth gave a decisive shake of her head in the negative to what Charlotte suggested.

"Lady Catherine will silence her staff. She wishes to keep Mr. Darcy for Miss De Bourgh. All will be well."

Charlotte flashed her a dry glance.

"Surely my intelligent friend Elizabeth Bennet realizes the foolhardiness of such hopes."

"But I..." Elizabeth began; yet, she did not finish.

"I realize you do not affect Mr. Darcy, but cultivate a liking for the man. Perhaps instead of an engagement, you might consider an understanding. Permit Mr. Darcy the opportunity to court you properly. Allow yourself time to discover Mr. Darcy's admirable qualities. Surely Mr. Bingley's opinion of the man holds some sway with you." Charlotte paused for emphasis. "If you find nothing in Mr. Darcy to induce you to marry him, an understanding is easier to terminate than an engagement."

Darcy did not go far; in misery, he clung to the wall outside Elizabeth's door and listened as Mrs. Collins skillful manipulated of Miss Elizabeth. The arrangement Mrs. Collins carved out would not be as he wished, but it would be a crack in Elizabeth's defenses. Darcy closed his eyes and brought forth an image of Elizabeth Bennet–his favorite–the one of her upon the stairs at Pemberley. The cinnamon of her hazel eyes rested purely upon him. The way his fingers reached for the silky firmness of her skin. The scent of lavender filling the air. How she moved with certainty and never with vanity. *Yet, Elizabeth is repulsed by the thought of your touch,* his foolish heart warned.

"He ruined Jane's chances," Elizabeth wailed. "And what of Mr. Wickham's hopes?"

"Wickham?" Darcy whispered silently. "Did Mr. Wickham hold the same hopes as I? Did George Wickham wish to claim Miss Elizabeth as his wife?" Darcy swallowed yet another dose of humiliation.

Mrs. Collins replied cryptically.

"Mr. Wickham's hopes are not what is important at this time, and as to Jane and Mr. Bingley demand that Mr. Darcy find a means to a reconciliation between his friend and Miss Bennet. It would be an excellent test of Mr. Darcy's affections and prove the gentleman has the mettle to admit the error of his decisions."

A long silence followed, and Darcy could almost hear Elizabeth contemplate if she could escape to Scotland or America rather than face him and her family.

"Ask Mr. Darcy to rejoin us," Elizabeth instructed, at length, her tone muffled.

Darcy made no attempt to hide when Mrs. Collins entered the passageway. Elizabeth's friend placed her finger to her lips and waited in silence. Finally, she signaled their return, and Darcy respectfully followed the woman into Elizabeth's room. The ploy was a poor one, and Darcy held no delusions Elizabeth thought he waited in one of the nearby sitting rooms. They each knew their roles in the charade they played.

"Mrs. Collins informs me you wish to speak to me."

"Mrs. Collins speaks with reason," Elizabeth demurred, "and if your offer remains, I would…" She paused as if in anguish. "I would reconsider; however, I would propose a slight modification–an understanding rather than an engagement. Would this be acceptable, Mr. Darcy?"

Elizabeth always was the most unguarded creature he ever met, but their connection changed her. It frightened Darcy to think so.

"How long?" For the first time since his early years as Pemberley's master, Darcy felt uncertainty, and it was not an emotion in which he took pleasure. "How long will the understanding last? How long must I wait to know you as my wife?"

The snarl of disdain that crossed Elizabeth's expression did little to improve Darcy's temperament.

"Three months. Six," she murmured.

"One, Miss Elizabeth," he negotiated, as if their life together was a business transaction. "One for an understanding. And then the banns will be called. Seven weeks. Agreed?"

Desperate situations required a desperate response. Darcy prayed two months would be long enough to persuade Elizabeth to care for him.

Elizabeth swallowed hard. Her bottom lip trembled when she spoke.

"Agreed, Mr. Darcy, but I possess an additional concession." Darcy studied Elizabeth's upturned countenance, seeking the answer to the question of finally knowing her. Her eyes darkened with annoyance. "Family is the reason I provided us this opportunity to come together, as such you should know I could never give my hand or my heart to a man who purposely divided my sister from Mr. Bingley, exposing one to censure of the world for caprice and instability, and the other to its derision for disappointed hopes." Elizabeth's chin wobbled for a second, but there was no improbability in her tone.

"It is not as if I did not know regret for my part in Bingley's distress," Darcy said lamely. "Yet, it must be noted that my interference may no longer be welcomed."

"A reconciliation between Mr. Bingley and Jane, Mr. Darcy," she insisted. "Or no engagement."

Not for the first time, Darcy wondered if winning the heart of the woman relaxing against the pillows was worth swallowing his pride a second time. For a moment, he considered walking away from Elizabeth's challenge–after all, she would be the one to know the world's disdain.

Word of Darcy's moving to protect her would elevate his status in Society's eyes. Yet, Darcy was not a faint-hearted man.

"If I am unsuccessful, Miss Elizabeth, it will not be for a lack of effort."

"As I am certain Lady Catherine expressed her displeasure with your arrangement," Mrs. Collins interrupted, "it is time for Elizabeth to withdraw from Hunsford. Mr. Collins is likely to suffer Her Ladyship's displeasure for his cousin's actions, and it would be best if Lizzy were not present to bring more ire upon my husband's head."

"Miss Elizabeth is in no condition to travel," Darcy protested.

"Perhaps not to Hertfordshire, but surely with an ample dose of laudanum, Elizabeth could withstand a journey to London. It is less than twenty miles."

"Even with my sister presence, it would be improper for Miss Elizabeth to reside at Darcy House," Darcy reasoned.

"I was thinking of Gracechurch Street," Mrs. Collins admitted. "With the Gardiners. Does Miss Bennet not remain in London?"

"Being with my dearest family would do me well, Mr. Darcy, and I long missed Jane's company," Elizabeth conceded.

It bothered Darcy that Elizabeth agreed so quickly: It was as if she anticipated her "escape" to London with too much joy. Did Elizabeth think when she reached her uncle's house she could put Darcy off? Or worse, did his future wife hope to arrange a reunion with Mr. Wickham?

"If it is your wish, Miss Elizabeth, then it is mine

also. I will make the necessary arrangements."

Mrs. Collins added several drops of laudanum to the tepid tea remaining in Elizabeth's glass.

"Drink this down, all at once. I know your aversion to the taste of the medicinal; however, it is time you found some rest. The remainder of the details of your arrangement with Mr. Darcy may be discussed over the next few days. Maria and I will take turns sitting with you this evening. With your permission, Lizzy, I will pack your belongings."

"It is so much bother, Charlotte."

"Never a bother for a friend," Mrs. Collins assured.

Darcy assumed Mrs. Collins's position beside Elizabeth's bed. Hearing her earlier objections to his touch, perversely, Darcy meant to assess Elizabeth's mettle.

"May I beg the favor of a kiss to seal our arrangement?" Darcy certainly did not want their first kiss to occur before an audience, but he liked the idea of testing Elizabeth as Elizabeth tested him: A challenge for a challenge. Somehow, Darcy thought he would enjoy her acquiescence more than Elizabeth had his. A slight nod indicated her agreement.

Obstinately, Darcy bent over her, savoring the warmth of her breath upon his cheek and the slight hitch in Elizabeth's breathing. It was quite satisfying to realize Elizabeth was not completely immune to his presence. Darcy lowered his head ever so slowly-tempting her desire, as well as his. When he knew Elizabeth ripe for his kiss, Darcy brushed her cheek with his lips.

Darcy stood quickly before he forgot himself and kissed Elizabeth Bennet until she moaned his name.

"Come along, Mrs. Collins. Miss Elizabeth requires

her rest." He caught her friend's elbow and directed the woman from the room. Closing the door behind him, Darcy could not quite stifle the smile, which tugged at the corners of his lips.

"Quite effective," Mrs. Collins sniggered. "Mr. Darcy, you will do quite well for my friend. Elizabeth has her immovable moments, but her heart is golden."

Darcy halted their steps.

"You earned my deepest gratitude, Mrs. Collins. I do not believe Miss Elizabeth would be so easily swayed by my words."

"You had two purposes in that semi-chaste kiss, Mr. Darcy," Mrs. Collins accused good-naturedly.

"And that would be?" Darcy asked with an answering grin.

"You tested Lizzy's indifference to you and found my friend's heart more engaged than she realizes."

"From your lips to God's ears, Mrs. Collins," Darcy whispered. "And the other reason."

"You have a witness to Elizabeth's permitting her own ruination." Darcy nodded his agreement. "Lizzy deserves love. Tell me you affect her, Mr. Darcy," the woman said softly, "and I will serve you gladly."

Darcy thought to deny his emotions; after all, a man possessed his pride, shredded as it may be, but Darcy knew the woman before him could prove a powerful ally. He closed his eyes to bring Elizabeth's image forth again.

"Most violently," he murmured.

"It is as I suspected," Mrs. Collins declared. "May I be permitted another observation, Mr. Darcy."

He shrugged his shoulders noncommittally.

"As you wish."

Moving a fraction closer, the lady lowered her voice further.

"Thinking he would be serving his family honorably, it will be difficult to delay Mr. Collins's sending word to Longbourn of Lizzy's injury and of your *arrangement* with my friend. It would be to your benefit to secure not only Mr. Bennet's permission to marry Lizzy, but also his active support. Elizabeth is excessively fond of her father and would hold his opinion most dear. Send Lizzy to London while you ride to Longbourn. You should inform Mr. Bennet of the change in Elizabeth's status rather than permitting Longbourn's master to learn of your impending marriage through one of my husband's eloquent letters."

As Darcy rode into the circle before Longbourn, his mind remained upon his parting from Elizabeth earlier in the day. With Mrs. Collins's exit, Darcy consulted with the colonel, and his cousin hardily agreed with the idea of departing Rosings the following morning.

"Certainly, I am capable of escorting Miss Elizabeth to London. I have no desire to remain in Kent with Aunt Catherine in a dudgeon. Plus, returning to Town will provide me the opportunity to seek out our thief. There are few places locally which would accept either your coat or the pistol in pawn."

Darcy agreed with his cousin's observations. In truth, Darcy had given little thought to the lost letter. All his energies rested with claiming Elizabeth Bennet.

"With Mrs. Collins's recommendation, I hired a girl from the village to travel with Miss Elizabeth and tend her in the carriage. The girl works in the millinery trade in London and is anxious to return to her position. She will be grateful not to suffer the mail coach."

Early this morning, Darcy oversaw Elizabeth's care before he set out for Hertfordshire.

"Lift her gently," Darcy instructed his footman after Darcy climbed into the carriage to accept Elizabeth's form from the man.

"I am well, Mr. Darcy," Elizabeth said in impatience.

"Humor me, Miss Elizabeth," he said as he shifted her to recline upon the forward-facing seat and placed a small pillow under her ankle to minimize the jostling motion of the coach. With purpose, Darcy lingered over Elizabeth before sitting back upon his heels. "I apologize for the use of my small coach. If I knew we were to return to London so soon, I would have sent for my traveling carriage."

Elizabeth smiled at him with that familiar hint of a tease, and Darcy braced for her barb.

"I am proud of you, Mr. Darcy. You expressed disdain without placing blame."

Darcy's foolish heart leapt with expectation.

"An education comes after one forgets what he once learned at university." Darcy spread a rug across her lap.

"I mean to call upon your father today to allay his concerns regarding your injury, as well as to inform him of the truth rather than to learn what occurred from Mr. Collins." He tucked the lap rug tight about Elizabeth's legs. "I asked Miss Lucas to accompany you, but the girl wished to remain with Mrs. Collins. I suspect your friend kept Miss Lucas in Kent in order to stifle the rumors while we manage our relationship." Darcy paused, uncertain whether Elizabeth would approve of his high-handedness. "I will ask your father to speak to Sir William regarding the return of his daughter."

Elizabeth's voice was stiff with pride when she responded.

"You acted prudently, and I appreciate your efforts to protect my reputation."

Darcy could not wipe the smile from his lips.

"As you requested, I confessed my 'sins' to Bingley. My missive was sent early this morning." Darcy accepted the bonnet she removed and placed it upon the opposing bench.

Suspicion laced Elizabeth's tone.

"You are being excessively attentive, Mr. Darcy."

"With a bit of luck, you will soon be part of my family, Miss Elizabeth, and despite what you may believe, I am built to protect my family from harm." He was on his knees before her; it would be so easy to lean in and steal a kiss, but Darcy would not risk the fragile truce resting between them.

A raised eyebrow of skepticism announced Elizabeth's request before she spoke the words.

"Tell me of yourself, Mr. Darcy. Speak of something no one else knows, not even your family."

Realizing this could be a moment of triumph if he chose well, Darcy searched for something significant, but not confrontational. They had come full circle, an irony, which did not escape him.

He edged closer to whisper in Elizabeth's ear.

"By most standards, I would be named a success. I learned to do what propriety requires, but I never learned what I should feel. Sometimes I believe I was born old, and I missed my youth. I am often intolerant with the negligible chatter of others, and until I took your acquaintance, I saw no end to the preordained steps of my life. I want a family, Elizabeth, a noisy, boisterous household where I might play soldier with my son or take my daughter ice-skating. Tell me this is not your dearest wish also."

Elizabeth's frown lines deepened, and Darcy wondered if he spoke his most private thoughts too soon.

"If your wish lies elsewhere, Elizabeth, I will do all in my power to make your dream a reality." He could possibly release her to another, but Darcy prayed her choice would not be Mr. Wickham. He doubted he could be so benevolent as to watch Elizabeth marry George Wickham. "Releasing you would be difficult, but we will play our roles, and after a proper time, we will tell everyone we did not suit."

Darcy could tell the laudanum Mrs. Collins insisted upon Elizabeth consuming claimed Elizabeth's quick reply. She nodded her understanding, while tears misted her eyes. With hard earned control, Darcy did not reach for her.

"Thank you, Mr. Darcy," Elizabeth said on a stifled sob.

Darcy could not quite leave her; it was exquisite torture to remain in Elizabeth's presence.

"Could you call me 'William'? 'Fitzwilliam' if you wish to be more formal. With the colonel being 'Fitzwilliam' also, my family chose 'Will' or 'William' for me."

Bewilderment shrouded Elizabeth's eyes, and when she spoke Darcy realized the medicinal affected her thoughts and her speech.

"How many children, Mr. Darcy?" she murmured, her words slurred. "Shall your son be a 'Fitzwilliam' also?" Her breath escaped a bit too quickly, and a blush infused Elizabeth's cheeks.

"I hoped if we should be so blessed that a son of our joining would assume his mother's surname–to take the customary form of 'Bennet,'" Darcy confessed.

Elizabeth's hand willingly sought his, and Darcy exulted in her touch.

"I would enjoy that fact very much, Mr. Darcy. I mean, William. I always thought it should be I to honor my father. I know it is Jane's domain as the eldest, but..."

Darcy understood perfectly: Elizabeth was Mr. Bennet's favorite.

Mr. Bennet's voice brought Darcy from his musings. He looked up as Elizabeth's father entered the Longbourn sitting room.

"Mr. Darcy? What brings you to Hertfordshire, Sir?"

Darcy sucked in a deep breath to steady his composure.

"I rode from Kent this day. I thought it important, Sir, to bring you the news Miss Elizabeth was injured."

Mrs. Bennet gasped, but Darcy kept his eyes on Elizabeth's father.

"How bad?" Bennet's lips trembled.

"Your daughter accidentally stepped in a trapper's lure, but she will not be maimed by the trap. I would have escorted your daughter to Longbourn, but Miss Elizabeth knows much discomfort. My cousin, Colonel Fitzwilliam, shepherded your daughter to Gracechurch Street while I delivered the news to your household."

Mr. Bennet nodded, but the man's frown lines deepened.

"Gracechurch was an excellent choice."

Darcy was aware of Bennet's unasked question of why it was necessary to remove Elizabeth from Rosings Park.

"It was a suggestion from Mrs. Collins, and I made the appropriate arrangements."

Bennet absorbed what Darcy disclosed.

"Mrs. Bennet's brother will see to Lizzy, and Jane is in London also." Without removing the cynicism from his tone, Elizabeth's father said, "We are indebted to you for the kindness you showed Lizzy, but a courier would have served the purpose just as well."

Darcy recognized Mr. Bennet as the source of Elizabeth's quick intelligence: It would not be easy to satisfy the man's curiosity. Darcy released his breath in a sigh of resignation.

"I assume you will soon receive a post from Mr. Collins, one detailing what occurred under Lady Catherine's roof: I thought my coming here would allay your qualms more efficiently than other means."

He noted the twitch of amusement upon Mr. Bennet's lips.

"I will anticipate the joy of reading my cousin's letter. Mr. Collins is quite articulating."

Darcy did not permit the man more whimsy.

"I hold other pressing business, Mr. Bennet, if you would spare me the luxury of your time."

Without enthusiasm, Elizabeth's father led Darcy to a book-cluttered study.

"I was not aware you were in Kent, Mr. Darcy," Bennet said without subtly before Darcy could assume a seat.

"It is my custom to call upon my aunt around Lady's Day to oversee her books for the year."

"Were you aware of Elizabeth's presence in Kent when you traveled there?"

Needless to say, Mr. Bennet guessed Darcy's purpose in seeking a private conference with the man.

Darcy would prefer not to feel as if the headmaster called Darcy before him, but Darcy responded with as much honesty as he could muster.

"Not until Her Ladyship informed me of it upon my arrival. Miss Elizabeth shared the news of our previous acquaintance with Lady Catherine, and my aunt knew curiosity with the connection."

"But you were not disappointed to discover my daughter residing with the Collinses?"

"I was not."

Mr. Bennet remained stubbornly silent for several minutes, but the quiet did not break Darcy. He was accustomed to serious negotiations, and Darcy long ago perfected the use of silence to his advantage.

"I suppose you should tell me what occurred between you and Elizabeth, Mr. Darcy. I am not of the nature to speculate on the welfare of my dearest child, but what I know of you, you are a man of honor."

"I pray when I finish my recitation you will

maintain your opinion of me, Sir."

It was the most excruciating two hours of Darcy's life; yet, he met each of Mr. Bennet's objections with calm reason and assurances. Having accepted Mrs. Collins's advice, Darcy held nothing close to his chest. He spoke of his desire to marry Elizabeth and of his shame at permitting his need to see her safe placing her in a compromised situation, but not of his prospects because, much as his daughter did, Mr. Bennet would consider such claims as false pride.

Bennet spoke in earnest of his reservations at losing Elizabeth to any man, but he acknowledged Darcy as an excellent match. "My Elizabeth is not of the same temperament as the others," Bennet declared. "Upon first acquaintance, one assumes Elizabeth resolute, but, in truth, she is quite vulnerable. Lizzy spent years telling anyone who would listen she has no desire to fulfill her duties as a wife and a mother or of taking a subservient role to her husband. My daughter based her opinions upon less-than-glowing examples." Darcy understood the man meant Bennet's marriage to Mrs. Bennet. "Elizabeth never permitted herself the dream of duty being excessively delightful when it comes at the hands of a person she affects."

Chapter 4

IT WAS MORE THAN four and twenty hours since Darcy placed Elizabeth in his coach, and he sorely missed her. He had with practiced graciousness accepted Mr. Bennet's offer of lodging for the evening. Surprisingly, Darcy enjoyed himself with the man; they exchanged barbs regarding politics and spent a great deal of time discussing tenants and crop rotations. Even Mrs. Bennet remained somewhat subdued to know her second daughter and he came to an understanding.

Now, Darcy stormed the steps of his Town home.

"Did all go well in Hertfordshire?" Georgiana asked when she met him in the family quarters. When he sent his missive to Bingley, he drafted a letter to his sister to explain the change in his prospects.

"As well as could be expected." Darcy tore at his cravat, tossing it on the back of a chair. "I will explain more later." He stepped around his sister. "Please pardon me; I know you have a multitude of questions, but I mean to make a quick call upon Miss Elizabeth. Her father sent her a written message. I promise not to tarry-just stay long enough to be assured of her continued recovery."

Georgiana blocked his passing.

"William, the colonel reports Miss Elizabeth took a turn for the worse. By the time he reached her uncle's house, Elizabeth possessed a high fever and did not respond to the colonel's urging. I am fearful, William. Your hopes may be quashed before they know fruition. We are both aware of the dangers of a fever; father did not survive his." It was a shared fear: George Darcy was healthy one day, and the next he was gone. Neither Darcy nor his sister expected such an outcome for their beloved patriarch, and the event played hard with their sensibilities. "Miss Bennet promised to send word, but no message has arrived."

Darcy caught at the back of a chair for support. He could still lose Elizabeth.

"Tell Mr. Gabriel I will take the horse again. There is no time to prepare the coach. I must be to Cheapside immediately. Hurry, Georgiana."

He did a poor job of tying a fresh cravat about his neck, but Darcy ignored his valet's efforts to correct the simply tied knot. Within a half hour, he rapped soundly upon the Gardiners' door.

"Yes, Sir," a servant answered immediately.

"I am Mr. Darcy, Miss Elizabeth's betrothed. I wish to see her."

"Darcy?" He looked up to note Bingley's approach.

Darcy stepped past the stunned servant.

"Bingley," Darcy implored without even the courtesy of a bow of greeting. "What can you tell me of

Miss Elizabeth's condition?"

Bingley judiciously guided Darcy into an empty sitting room.

"The colonel summoned a physician with whom he was familiar after he realized the seriousness of Miss Elizabeth's condition."

The news brought Darcy up short. His mind scrambled for a logical explanation for the turn of events.

"Please tell me the physician was in time."

"Mr. Morton removed a sliver of the cloth from one of the puncture wounds," Bingley continued. "The piece of material was nothing more than a few fine threads, but they were large enough to cause an infection. We are praying the contagion does not spread. Miss Bennet sent a dispatch to her father to apprise Mr. Bennet of this turn of events."

"I departed Longbourn early this morning," Darcy said lamely.

Bingley cleared his throat in embarrassment.

"Your letter was quite a shock, Darcy. I do not know whether to be angry with you for being a part of the sorrow delivered to Miss Bennet's door or to be grateful you found the courage to admit what occurred."

Deep in thoughts of Elizabeth, Darcy spoke in distraction.

"I should have acted sooner. I promised Miss Elizabeth to set things aright." He looked steadily upon his companion. "It was poor of me to act against your will."

"It was contemptuous," Bingley agreed. "But Miss Bennet says it would be a betrayal of Miss Elizabeth's wishes if we did not forgive."

Instant regret arrived. Darcy severely wronged his dearest friend, as well as Miss Bennet, and indirectly Elizabeth. Although he swore he would protect Elizabeth, Darcy permitted his jealousy and his pettiness in his dealings with Bingley and with Wickham to override his reason where Elizabeth was concerned. He agreed with the Bingley sisters because Darcy knew he could not remain Bingley's confidant if his friend married Miss Bennet. Likely, Bingley would insist Darcy stand up with him. Darcy could not consider seeing Elizabeth Bennet with another. He would be forced to break all ties with Bingley.

"I must see her," Darcy pressed.

Bingley scowled his disapproval.

"It would be everything impolite, Darcy."

"I asked Miss Elizabeth to share my life," Darcy pleaded. Bingley's features settled into an unreadable expression, but Darcy pressed, "I am certain you are acquainted with some of what occurred between Miss Elizabeth and me, but I assure you I always acted with Elizabeth first in my mind and my heart. Think upon it, Bingley. When have you known me to respond without prudence?" It unsettled Darcy to beg, but beg he would if it moved him closer to Elizabeth. "I am certain your presence in Cheapside announces the continuation of your affections for Miss Bennet." Urgency nearly chocked Darcy. "Tell me, Bingley: What would you do if the woman above were Miss Bennet? Would you sit idly by because propriety demanded it? Or would you tell Society's strictures to take flight in order to be by your lady's side?"

"Bloody hell, Darcy!" Bingley expelled. "You are

in love."

Darcy nodded his affirmation curtly.

"Assist me, Bingley, or I will not be held responsible for my actions."

Bingley chuckled and slapped Darcy good-naturedly on the shoulder.

"Wait here. I shan't be long."

Within minutes, his friend returned to the room with Miss Bennet and a middle-aged matron.

"Mr. Darcy, may I present Mrs. Gardiner? Mrs. Gardiner, my friend Mr. Darcy, Miss Elizabeth's affianced."

Darcy exchanged courtesies with the handsome woman, who studied him most carefully. She was several years Mrs. Bennet's junior and carried herself as if raised in the finest of homes.

"I understand you wish to call upon Lizzy. I fear my husband's niece is not conscious: She will not be aware of your presence," Mrs. Gardiner assured.

With a stab of exasperation, Darcy vowed, "Nevertheless, I insist, Mrs. Gardiner."

A deep sadness flickered across the woman's expressive countenance.

"Very well, Mr. Darcy. Follow me."

As he passed his friend standing dutifully beside Elizabeth's sister, Darcy turned to whisper.

"Do not deny yourself even one day of happiness with Miss Bennet. Declare your intentions, Bingley, and claim your perfect mate. Fate has a cruel sense of humor, and tomorrow could be too late."

In less than a minute, Darcy knelt beside Elizabeth's bed–first in prayer, pleading to God for her recovery, and then to catch her hand in his. She appeared so frail. So delicate. What happened to the woman who challenged him only a day prior? Was she ill, even then? A frighteningly intense pain stabbed his heart: He failed her as assuredly as he failed Georgiana. The devil take it, he could not bear to lose her. Elizabeth Bennet made a mare's nest of his normally astute mind, and he could not meekly wait to learn of her demise. A moment of pain he knew but twice previously sent panic coursing through Darcy's veins.

He nuzzled her cold fingertips with his lips.

"Do not leave us, Elizabeth." A tempest of need and longing and fear stormed his heart. "I meant what I said previously: I will see you with a man whose opinions and dreams are as far-reaching as your own, even if that man is not I. The world cannot continue to exist without your spirit in it, Elizabeth Bennet, and I cannot live without knowing you are happy in your chosen life."

Elizabeth rocked forth and back in the bed, and a moan escaped her lips.

"You must return to us, my love." He brushed a curl from her cheek. "Hope returned to your sister's features, and you must observe it for yourself. It would not exist if you did not take me to task."

Many evenings Darcy sat in his private quarters at Darcy House and argued with his conscience regarding his actions in Bingley's behalf. He knew from the beginning, he erred. Yet, looking upon Elizabeth's pale countenance brought Darcy's pride to a stumbling halt. How could he slip so far from the path his father carved out for him? Had it been youthful self-absorption, which made Darcy think he was above the Bennets? At an age

Mr. Darcy's Fault

barely beyond his majority, he inherited his father's power, and Darcy used it to keep Pemberley thriving; but somewhere along the way, he lost himself. He assumed his father's mannerisms, but, in truth, Darcy was more of his mother's nature. Although Lady Anne Darcy knew her moments of privilege, his mother taught him forbearance and simple gratitude, but Darcy quashed those traits in order to survive in a man's world.

He smiled as Elizabeth's mouth twisted in a familiar pout. The woman certainly turned Darcy's world upon its head. She was beautiful, but that was not the reason he sought Elizabeth out. She filled his soul in a most inhospitable manner, one he never expected. Whenever Darcy looked upon her, a longing he could never describe in words or actions would take hold of his insides. It was a storm of need he could not control.

He bent to kiss her wrist.

"You are my bane, Elizabeth Bennet." Her head was turned from him, and Darcy could look upon the length of her neck. Without thought, his eyes searched for the pulse point at the base of the slender column. How many times did he dream of running his lips along her skin? Now, he was simply happy to note the steady pulsation. Darcy caught a damp cloth resting on a basin of water to wipe her cheeks and wrists. "Please, Elizabeth," he pleaded. "I cannot bear to see you suffer." Over and over he wiped the sweat from her forehead. Darcy had no idea how long he sat beside her until Miss Bennet touched his shoulder.

"Elizabeth is strong, Mr. Darcy," she whispered. "You must have faith in her."

Darcy did not remove his eyes from Elizabeth's

tortured countenance. He trailed a fingertip up her arm and down again.

"You will think me mad, Miss Bennet. Your sister tempts my heart in a manner no one else ever will. Elizabeth must recover, or I shall remain unwed."

"Mr. Darcy," Jane Bennet argued. "Although I hold no doubt Elizabeth will recover, you must consider your estate. If God in His infinite wisdom chooses to claim Elizabeth as one of his angels, my sister would wish you to know happiness. Elizabeth would not wish to be the reason for your sorrow."

Darcy stood slowly, knowing propriety would drive him from Elizabeth's side.

"Nevertheless, I mean to have Elizabeth as my wife or no one." He turned to her sister. "You will send word if there is a change in Miss Elizabeth's condition. Do not have a care of the hour. I will not sleep until I am certain this setback turns toward the better. With your permission, I will return tomorrow morning."

"Certainly."

Darcy permitted Miss Bennet to direct him to the door, but when he glanced back for one last look upon Elizabeth's countenance, her head was turned in his direction, and her eyes were open wide.

"William?" she rasped.

Immediately, Darcy was at her side, crossing the room in four long strides.

"Yes. I am here. We are at Gracechurch Street. Your sister and Mr. Bingley and your aunt and uncle." He clutched Elizabeth's hand to his chest.

"And you," she whispered through dry lips.

"Wherever you are Elizabeth Bennet, so will I be,"

Darcy said as he brushed the hair from her forehead. Although she was still warm to his touch, her fever was down. "It is imperative you do not forsake your fight against this fever. Do you understand me, Elizabeth? You must place all your energies in returning to your family." *Returning to me*, he thought.

"Family." Her breathlessness spoke of Elizabeth's exhaustion.

"Yes, family," he assured. "Your family. Our family." Elizabeth closed her eyes and slipped back into sleep, but Darcy noted the slight upward curl of the corners of her lips. He kissed her knuckles and stood again to stare down upon her. Elizabeth made the effort to assure him of her resolve. She was far from safe, but a flicker of hope arrived. "Keep me informed, Miss Bennet. I will call after the breakfast hour. I will sit with Elizabeth until she is well."

It was on the third day of her confinement before Elizabeth remained awake for more than a few minutes. Each day, Darcy dutifully sat beside her bed. Her Uncle Gardiner objected in no uncertain terms to Darcy's presence in his niece's rooms, but Darcy refused to do anything less. It was as if he convinced himself as long as he could watch over her, Elizabeth would survive.

"She needs me," he explained to Georgiana after the second day of his vigil. "I doubt Miss Elizabeth would acknowledge the possibility, but I feel it nonetheless. I sound mad, do I not?"

Fortunately, his sister's tender heart understood.

"Do what you must to see Miss Elizabeth well. I long desired a sister."

"You remain." Elizabeth said weakly as she lifted her head to glance about the room. "Where is Jane?"

Darcy rose to assist her to a seated position.

"Your sister stepped from the room. Miss Bennet wished to apprise your father of your continued improvement, but she required ink for her pen." When Elizabeth was settled, Darcy returned to his chair. "How feel you?"

Elizabeth licked her dry lips.

"As if a coal cart knocked me from its way." Elizabeth attempted to comb her hair with her fingers, but to little avail.

"Shall I send to the kitchen for some clear broth? You have had nothing to eat since the day we departed Kent."

"In a moment." She eyed him steadily. "Have you been home, Sir?"

Moderating the hitch in his breathing Elizabeth's warm gaze created in him, Darcy managed to say, "Your uncle frowned upon the idea of my remaining throughout the night."

Elizabeth's fingers ran along the stitching upon the blanket across her chest.

"Why?" she asked so softly Darcy would have missed the question if he were not listening carefully. There was a bittersweet echo of loneliness in Elizabeth's tone, and Darcy recalled Mr. Bennet speaking of Elizabeth's vulnerability.

Darcy smiled with ease.

"I suppose you are not inquiring as to why your uncle would object to my spending the night in your quarters."

Elizabeth's tone pierced the tight silence between them.

"Why would you remain with me? I treated you quite poorly in our past."

"Not true," Darcy denied. "I find your obstinacy enticing." He winked at Elizabeth. Darcy could not recall a time when he thought to flirt with a woman. In Society, he fended off such maneuverings from innocent maids trained by their mamas in stratagems to claim a husband.

"You think we are alike," Elizabeth claimed baldly.

Darcy wondered where this conversation would lead, hopefully not to another confrontation.

"In many ways."

Again, Elizabeth flicked her fingers through the tangles in her locks.

"Such as?"

Darcy smothered the urge to smile.

"We…we both possess strong allegiances to family. We are the ones upon whom the others depend." Elizabeth silently nodded her agreement. "We are often from step with what is required of us in polite society." Darcy shrugged his shoulders in self-acceptance. "I more so than you."

"Neither of us speak with false platitudes," Elizabeth said quietly.

"Nay, and I am certain it is as for you as it is for me: Knowing regret even when you believe your opinions the most sensible choice."

The candlelight caught the red strains of her hair, making it appear as if full of sparks.

Elizabeth's smile was fierce.

"We have said hateful things."

"Our individual pride knew its day." All they once said to each other laid the bricks for a new understanding. "I doubt if either of us ever spoke so harshly to another," Darcy ventured. In truth, he thought her waspish words were a sign of Elizabeth's deep passions.

"Perhaps thought it," she said with a familiar flippancy.

Darcy's mood changed subtly.

"Perhaps so. I can attest to a very difficult merchant in Lambton I often wished to the devil."

Trusting and open, Elizabeth replied, "I wished you there also."

Darcy smiled as his chest permitted a bit of hope in.

"I imagine you will do so again. I am often singular in my opinions."

"I noted that particular quality, Sir."

They were back on familiar ground. A verbal swordplay. Feint and retreat. Charge and thrust. Yet, a common dream rested between them.

"You bring out the best in me, Miss Elizabeth. I told my sister exactly that only yesterday."

Chapter 5

IT TOOK ELIZABETH NEARLY a week before she stood with any ease upon her injured foot; even then, Darcy noted her stride had shortened. After their "truce," Darcy took to calling in the afternoons. Mr. Gardiner's staff would carry Elizabeth down from the bedroom, and he and she would sit together, usually devouring the many newsprints he brought with him for Elizabeth's entertainment: Her quick mind sought answers to more than what Lady So-and-So wore to last evening's ball. They discussed politics, the war, investments, and land acquisition, and with each revealing conversation, Darcy realized how truly blessed he would be if Elizabeth Bennet agreed to be his wife.

"Miss Elizabeth." He bowed as Darcy entered the sitting room to which Gardiner's servant led him. "I am pleased to note a bit more color in your cheeks today. You are looking well."

Elizabeth blushed, and Darcy thought he never

saw her look more becoming.

"Thank you, Sir." She struggled to her feet to greet him. When Darcy reached to support her, Elizabeth stayed him with a flick of her wrist. Her determination returned, and Darcy celebrated the moment: Elizabeth was truly on the mend.

Attempting to conceal the rapid pace of his heart, Darcy gestured to the girl standing off his shoulder.

"As you gave me permission to act, I brought my sister to take your acquaintance. "Miss Elizabeth Bennet, it is with pride I present my sister Miss Darcy."

Elizabeth smiled at the girl, who was as delicate as a porcelain doll in her appearance. Blonde, where Mr. Darcy was dark of head. Slender, but taller than she. Silky complexion untouched by the sun.

"Miss Elizabeth," the girl murmured sweetly. "My brother speaks often of you. It is pleasant finally to take your acquaintance."

Elizabeth glanced to the ever-brooding Mr. Darcy. The man appeared quite anxious of her reaction to his sister. *Does he expect me to shun the girl? Or was his anxiousness in fear I might say something crass and embarrass him?*

"Please come sit beside me, Miss Darcy," Elizabeth instructed. "Like you, I am pleased for us to learn more of each other."

Mr. Darcy bowed a second time.

"I will leave you. I promised Mr. Gardiner to bring him information upon the docking of the *Jupiter Star* this morning."

With suspicion, Elizabeth eyed Darcy.

"I was not aware you and Uncle Gardiner held joint business interests."

The man had the audacity to wink at her, and Elizabeth found the private gesture set her pulse racing.

"There are many aspects of my life of which your are unaware, Miss Elizabeth."

"But..." She waited for what remained of his quip. It was the way of them. They would challenge and retreat.

"In spite of your chary nature, there is nothing more." Elizabeth waited again; this time she expected a "my dear" or a "my girl" added to the end of the sentence; yet, none came. In many ways, not hearing the endearment disappointed her.

A bit irritated with her foolish heart, she responded waspishly.

"Be about your business, Mr. Darcy. Your sister and I will soon be well ensconced in our conversation."

As if he knew Elizabeth's thoughts, Mr. Darcy nodded his head in agreement.

"As you wish, my dear," and then he was gone.

Elizabeth turned happily to Darcy's sister. As she addressed the girl, Elizabeth refused to acknowledge the satisfaction of having Mr. Darcy's affection. Odd: Only a fortnight prior she would cringe at the thought.

"Tell me something of yourself, Miss Darcy."

Initially, the girl hemmed and hawed, but with a bit of encouragement, Miss Darcy enthusiastically described her life at Pemberley and in London. Elizabeth thought it ironic the way Miss Darcy described her brother as "the best."

"You cannot know how kind William is," the girl swore in sincerity. "He is too good to me."

Amused by Miss Darcy's naivety, Elizabeth half teased, "Surely, Mr. Darcy possesses some faults."

Miss Darcy's eyes grew in astonishment.

"I suppose those who participate in hard negotiations with my brother would hold a different opinion from I. William, after all, learned his lessons in business at our father's knee. Yet, my brother possesses a tender heart for those he affects."

"And what of those who earned Mr. Darcy's ire?"

Elizabeth could not seem to escape her doubts, those fueled of Mr. Wickham's accusations, in comparison with this new Mr. Darcy–the one who protected her throughout her illness.

Miss Darcy caught Elizabeth's hand.

"If I may be so bold, I do not believe you possess anything of which to worry, Miss Elizabeth. I never knew William to speak so highly of any woman."

Elizabeth wondered what Mr. Darcy said of her, but that was a question for another day.

"I am honored by your brother's attentions," Elizabeth declared, "but I was thinking of another. In Hertfordshire, my family took the acquaintance of Mr. Wickham, who had..."

Miss Darcy went perfectly still, all blood rushing from the girl's face and interrupting Elizabeth's maneuverings.

"Miss Darcy, have I said something to upset you?"

Elizabeth patted her new friend's wrist before placing the back of her hand against the girl's forehead. Miss Darcy attempted to rally her spirits, but Elizabeth could tell the girl struggled to keep her countenance with distress.

"Please," Miss Darcy whispered. "Do not ask me to speak of Mr. Wickham."

"Certainly not," Elizabeth assured. "If I knew my words would trouble you so, I would never have spoken. What Mr. Wickham said…"

The girl clawed at Elizabeth's hands.

"Did Mr. Wickham speak of me? Please say it cannot be."

Elizabeth brushed the hair from the girl's cheek.

"I promise no one uttered anything more than the fact Mr. Darcy possessed a younger sister for whom he served as guardian." Elizabeth stroked the back of the girl's hand. "We should speak of something more comfortable. Should I tell you a bit of my sisters? You will meet my eldest sister Jane when she returns from errands, but I have three others."

Miss Darcy squeezed away the tears misting her eyes.

"I would enjoy hearing of your family, Miss Elizabeth. I cannot imagine the pleasure of four sisters." Her tone was sincere, but hard emotions caused the girl's voice to crack twice.

"Pleasure is likely too strong a word, Miss Darcy," Elizabeth said with forced lightness to ease the Georgiana Darcy's qualms. It bothered Elizabeth not to possess an answer to the question, which would forever separate her and Mr. Darcy. Despite the inroads the gentleman made into Elizabeth's resolve, the nagging question of Mr. Darcy's cruel behavior toward his acknowledged childhood friend still loomed strong within Elizabeth's mind.

"*Is it possible Mr. Darcy is as two faced as Janus?*" she

asked her empty quarters as Elizabeth crawled into her bed. "Even Miss Darcy admitted her brother could be tenacious in his business dealings and was not the negotiation of a living a business matter?"

"Mr. Bingley?" Elizabeth lowered her voice so the maid, who rode upon the rear seat of the gentleman's curricle, could not overhear.

Bingley agreed to escort Elizabeth to a draper's shop where she was to meet Jane and their Aunt Gardiner. Nearly two weeks passed since Elizabeth awoke from her fever to discover Mr. Darcy watching over her–*three weeks tomorrow,* she thought, since she struck a bargain with Mr. Darcy for an understanding: a month of learning more of each other before they officially announced their engagement. Having conversed with the man each day since her recovery, her defenses weakened, but nagging doubts remained, and Elizabeth was unable to shake them.

"Would you be so good as to speak honestly of your current opinion of Mr. Darcy? My dearest Jane forgave the gentleman's offenses, but I would expect nothing less from my sister, who possesses the kindest of hearts."

Bingley smiled affably,

"And I do not?" Bingley teased.

Elizabeth struck his arm with her folded fan.

"No bamming me, Mr. Bingley," she warned good-naturedly.

The gentleman presented her a lop-sided grin.

"Certainly not, Miss Elizabeth." He maneuvered his curricle about a coal cart. "It is my intention of some day calling you 'sister.'"

Elizabeth, despite her best efforts, thought she would not like to think of Bingley's sisters claiming a like familiarity. Louisa Hurst and the callous Caroline Bingley would never speak fondly of her, and Elizabeth doubted she could ever offer more than cold politeness to those who treated Jane poorly. She held no doubt Miss Bingley would continue to present Elizabeth with venomous barbs because of Mr. Darcy's obvious attention.

"Do you hold objections to my doing so?"

To Elizabeth's dismay, a rush of blood flooded her cheeks. She realized the thought of Caroline Bingley brought a snarl of distaste to Elizabeth's nose.

"Lord, no," Elizabeth insisted. "I never observed Jane so content," she said with feeling. "But you avoid my question, Sir. What of your relationship with Mr. Darcy?"

A long silence followed, and Elizabeth thought perhaps Mr. Bingley would not respond.

"The months without your sister's company were the most difficult ones of my life. I cannot describe the depth of my despair." Bingley regarded Elizabeth in close examination before returning his gaze to the street traffic. "A man does not speak with ease of such feelings, Miss Elizabeth."

She wrapped her hand about Bingley's elbow.

"I am not asking you to verbalize your regard for my sister. Save your pretty words for Jane." For the length of several heartbeats, an odd sort of silence rested between Elizabeth and Bingley. "I suppose what I wish to know is whether you would ever trust Mr. Darcy with the care of your friendship again? I simply cannot think of accepting a man who blatantly disregarded a friend's loyalty."

Bingley's eyes glittered darkly.

"It would be the greatest falsehood if I claimed that I did not wish Darcy to Hades for his perfidy; yet, as painful as it was to read how he and my sisters plotted against me, as I reread Darcy's letter a second and a third time, I could give Darcy a bit of forgiveness. As my friend, he often heard me profess my "love" for this girl or that, and he possessed no means of knowing the depth of my attachment to Miss Bennet. Darcy knew how my early flirtations showed themselves as nothing more than the mist rolling in from the sea. They dissipated quickly. In truth, I acted ungentlemanly in my dealings with your sister for I did not give a fig about the general expectation of my Meryton neighbors. I should have acted with more prudence, and it was not chivalrous of me to demonstrate a lack of care for your sister's reputation."

Elizabeth never considered Mr. Bingley's response to Jane as anything but attentive attraction, but she kept her opinions private for the time being.

"In his letter, Darcy described how he set about watching Miss Bennet. And if I was honest, and in this case, it was necessary for me to be so, what my friend described was what I felt when conversing with your sister. Miss Bennet's look and manners were open, cheerful, and engaging, but I was constantly in turmoil as to whether your sister would welcome my regard."

"Jane is simply shy," Elizabeth protested.

Bingley peered at her more closely.

"I understand that particular fact now, but not so much when I first took your sister's acquaintance. Like it or not, Darcy did not believe Miss Bennet to be indifferent because he wished it to be so. Everything I know of Darcy says he would not act purely from hopes or fears. Caroline and Louisa might respond from conceit, but never Darcy. He is a man of reason. Darcy accepted my friendship when many of the *ton* chose to present me a direct cut. As a gentleman's daughter, Miss Bennet is above my status in Society. If anything, Darcy's objections were to keep me from reaching for the impossible."

Elizabeth did not like to dwell on such discrepancies, but she was not foolish enough to think others would not see the situation with a questioning gaze. Bingley's eyes softened.

"Have I completely forgiven Darcy for his involvement? No. Will I? Most definitely. And more importantly, would I trust Darcy again? I would, for in spite of his error, my friend acted to protect me. Very much as he did with you, Miss Elizabeth."

"With me?" Elizabeth sputtered. "Do you not think Mr. Darcy acted with high handedness?"

"Darcy placed himself between you and the gossips who would gladly belie your reputation. As Darcy's wife, you will hold great sway in Society. The man invested his future and that of his estate in your hands, Miss Elizabeth. Can you not see how deeply my friend admires you?"

"I observe a man accustomed to having things as he chooses them," Elizabeth said defiantly. "Mr. Darcy's insistence upon tending me when I was ill left me no choice but to marry him. If not, your connection to Jane would lose its luster."

"Even if you would choose to rush off to Gretna Green with another or to seek a life as a lady's companion rather than to marry Darcy," Bingley assured, "I would still insist upon marrying Miss Bennet. But I deal in goods and trade, and I am not so high in the instep as are many gentlemen." Bingley nodded in something resembling sullenness. "Can you truly find nothing in Darcy upon which to hitch your stars, Miss Elizabeth? You know, of course, he could have passed on the responsibility of your reputation to his cousin, the colonel, who volunteered to take you to wife to save Darcy the connection."

Elizabeth responded in dour tones.

"The colonel's offer was likely Lady Catherine's idea. I ruined her great plan to marry Mr. Darcy to Miss De Bourgh."

"Yes," Bingley smiled easily. "You upset Her Ladyship's apple cart, as sure as you did my sister's. But think upon what all occurred. You would be just as compromised if Darcy did nothing more than to free you from the trap or to carry you to safety. He did not need to remain by your side through long days and nights for Society to pressure you into marriage. Darcy tended you because his heart is engaged. I would do the same if the lady in the fits of fever were Miss Bennet. Can you not accept Darcy's kindness and build a lasting relationship?"

Elizabeth smiled weakly.

"I attempt to see my way clear, but so much remains unanswered."

"Then perhaps, my dear, you should spend your time with Darcy asking him for honest declarations. Plan your future together. Do not enter a marriage while doubt plagues your every thought. You will only know disappointment."

"Would you and Mr. Darcy care to join us?" Jane asked from the open door to the sitting room. "Mr. Bingley and I mean to stroll in the park."

Darcy shot Elizabeth an inquisitive look. From the moment he entered the sitting room Darcy recognized something troubled Elizabeth.

"I am a bit weary after our earlier outing. If Mr. Darcy holds no objections, I would prefer to spend time in Uncle Gardiner's garden."

"No objections whatsoever. I am at your disposal, Miss Elizabeth."

Darcy noted the questioning look from her sister, but although Miss Bennet and Bingley suspected Elizabeth's intent, no one indicated they knew Miss Elizabeth's plan.

With her sister's withdrawal, Darcy asked, "Is there something amiss?"

"Not at all." Elizabeth stood. "May we enjoy the bits of sun in uncle's garden?"

Darcy followed her to his feet.

"Certainly," he pronounced as he offered her his elbow. It bothered Darcy that Elizabeth would not meet his eyes. After she donned her bonnet to protect her complexion from the sun, Darcy directed her steps through the side entrance to the garden behind the Gardiners' Town house. Although her aunt and uncle resided in Cheapside, in close proximity to Edward Gardiner's warehouses, the Gardiner home displayed a touch of gentility.

Darcy seated Elizabeth upon a small bench and waited for what she would say to him. It did not slip Darcy's attention that they approached the one month deadline for which Darcy valiantly negotiated in Kent: Would this be the day Elizabeth Bennet would agree to be his wife or would she send him away, hat in hand?

Elizabeth stalled by straightening the seams of her dress. At length, she said, "Mr. Darcy, I thought long and hard upon what occurred in Kent and how the situation *forced* us into a…a joining."

Darcy wished he held a better view of her expression so he might judge her emotions, but Elizabeth's bonnet covered part of her features.

"I feel far from put upon, Miss Elizabeth, but I understand if you possess different opinions."

She glanced at him and frowned before Elizabeth dropped her eyes again.

"My objections have undergone somewhat of a change, but I believe we should speak in earnest of what occurred during our acquaintance."

Darcy's heart leapt with expectation. He prayed Elizabeth's heart might be softened in his favor, but the idea of "honesty" lacked appeal. He feared if she knew everything, the pendulum could swing in the opposite direction.

"I will endeavor to answer whatever questions you feel necessary."

Elizabeth continued without an acknowledgement of his response, and Darcy wondered if she rehearsed what she wished to say to him.

"We both are aware I was reading your letter when I stumbled into the trapper's lure. In truth, I read only as far as you outlined the charges I made against you: I did not read your explanations. I believe it prudent I hear them before we proceed. If you do not wish to repeat what you said previously, you might simply return the letter to me to read."

Darcy spared Elizabeth a brief, anguished glance. Unable not to look upon her countenance when he spoke of his affections for her, Darcy moved to kneel before her.

"I wish I never wrote that cursed letter. All it did was to bring you pain."

Elizabeth lifted her chin in a proud gesture.

"Are you saying you wish to forego our arrangement?"

"Never." Darcy smiled with kindness. "For months, I thought of little else."

"Then what are you suggesting?"

Darcy stiffened.

"In hindsight, my pride demanded I have my say. I chose my words and tone poorly: I sought satisfaction for the pang of regret I carried throughout the night."

"Neither of us acted with sensibility. If you will honor me with your confidences, I shall promise not to respond without logic," Elizabeth reasoned.

Darcy tilted his head to one side to study her features.

"I no longer am in possession of the letter."

Elizabeth appeared confused.

"Have you rid yourself of it? Did you burn in one of Lady Catherine's grates? I would understand if you preferred another not to read it. You may simply repeat your explanation aloud."

Darcy gave the back of Elizabeth's hand a gentle squeeze.

"I will do exactly that, but you should know the letter went missing."

"Missing?" Elizabeth's voice rose to a squeak.

Darcy's regrets at having acted so foolishly arrived.

"When you knew injury, all I thought was to see you safely to the manor. To make it easier to carry you to Rosings, I removed your cloak and my great coat and left them at the scene, along with the coat pistol I extracted from my person when I heard the dogs' call. I did not think to look for the letter."

"Certainly someone knows of the letter's whereabouts. My cloak was returned to you," Elizabeth reasoned.

Darcy hesitated: The image of the figure he sought in Rosings Woods rushed to the forefront.

"I asked Colonel Fitzwilliam to retrieve the items, including the letter, for I knew my cousin would act with discretion. Yet, Fitzwilliam returned from the scene with only your cloak and the broken cane I used to prevent the trap from reclaiming your ankle. My coat, the pistol, and the letter were no where to be found."

Elizabeth's ire, as well as her disbelief, grew.

"And what have you done about this intrusion into our privacy, Mr. Darcy?"

Darcy liked the word *our* in Elizabeth's question.

"I spoke privately with Lady Catherine's steward, head groundskeeper, and lead groom, insisting they send word if they uncovered any information. My cousin also spent countless hours searching for the items." Darcy realized the colonel meant to protect Georgiana, not Elizabeth, but the end would prove beneficial to both. "Within a ten mile radius of the estate, there was no word of a coat or the pistol offered for sale. Fitzwilliam has inquiries in many of the usual London establishments."

"Is the remainder of the letter so…"

"Damning," Darcy supplied. He thought of

Georgiana's future. "None of what is revealed is ideal, and others could lose face if the letter becomes public."

Elizabeth motioned Darcy to the seat at her side.

"I suspect you should confess all, Mr. Darcy, and we shall decide what action is required."

Chapter 6

IN HER SHORT LIFE, Elizabeth never spent a more difficult hour. She asked for Mr. Darcy's honesty, and she thought herself prepared, but Elizabeth's emotions knew a full assault. Even her breathing constricted. To look upon Mr. Darcy's ashen countenance brought a swell of longing to her chest.

Darcy spoke with painful regret when he described his objections to Mr. Bingley's connection to Jane. Very much as Mr. Bingley asserted earlier, the man who hoped to call Elizabeth "wife" labeled his actions as "misguided" by the serenity of Jane's expression when her sister looked upon Mr. Bingley.

"I thought Miss Bennet's heart not easily touched, and it grieves me to know I erred by inflicting pain upon her."

Elizabeth recalled Charlotte's remarking upon a like assumption, and although she thought both her dear friend and Mr. Darcy should practice more care in declaring Jane's heart indifferent, Elizabeth could understand how the two could misinterpret her dear sister's extreme shyness.

"In my conceit, in the letter I spoke of how I overcame my initial objections to your family, but please know I have..." A blush of embarrassment claimed Mr. Darcy's features.

He rushed to assure Elizabeth of his devotion, but she cut off Darcy's words of affection.

"I would hear those protestations, if you please, Mr. Darcy," Elizabeth insisted.

"Must I, Miss Elizabeth? I spoke with a superiority taught to me by my revered father, a sense of entitlement I never questioned until my aunt acted in such an abominable manner toward you as a guest in her parlor," he confessed.

Elizabeth shook her head in denial.

"If we are to know harmony in our relationship, Mr. Darcy, it is imperative no secrets lie between us." To lighten the mood, Elizabeth half teased, "You would not wish to present Miss Bingley the opportunity to offer me one of her 'sweet' barbs, would you, Sir?"

A sad smile turned down the corners of Mr. Darcy's lips.

"Never that." A silence settled between them. Finally, a clearing of the gentleman's throat announced Mr. Darcy's resolve to continue. "Since my apologies are not to your taste..." he murmured before stiffening his back as if entering a battle of wills. "First, permit me to say my censure never fell upon your or Miss Bennet's shoulders. I always spoke in praise of the sense and disposition you and your sister displayed." His point-by-point depiction of her mother's crass remarks to and about Darcy, as well as Mrs. Bennet's assumption that Jane would receive Mr. Bingley's proposal followed. Mr. Darcy included an observation of Lydia and Kitty's public pursuit of the officers of the regiment. He even noted her father's embarrassing Mary in the Netherfield music room.

Although Elizabeth did not wish to hear Mr. Darcy criticize her family's lack of manners, she conceded she held similar thoughts upon the night of the Netherfield ball. As it happens, after the supper hour, Elizabeth hid in the withdrawing room, unable to meet the scorn in Miss Bingley's and Mr. Darcy's eyes without breaking into tears at their unspoken accusations.

"Forgive me, Elizabeth," Mr. Darcy whispered as he encircled her in his arms.

Elizabeth realized the tears she hid at the ball now slipped down her cheeks. She thought to push the gentleman away, but instead Elizabeth caught Mr. Darcy's lapels and pulled him closer. His warmth and tenderness made her feel cherished in a manner she had not experienced since she was a small child upon her father's lap. Her father's favoring Elizabeth often sent Mrs. Bennet into a fit of the vapors.

"It is not proper, Mr. Bennet," her mother accused when Elizabeth scampered into her dearest papa's arms, "for you to permit our daughter such latitude and to show Lizzy the favor of your affection."

To quiet his wife's objections, Mr. Bennet placed Elizabeth on her feet and sent her to her room. Since that day, her father only demonstrated his affections in private.

Mr. Darcy slipped his handkerchief into her hand,

and Elizabeth dabbed at her eyes.

"You must think me a foolish watering pot," Elizabeth offered in apology.

"Believe me," Mr. Darcy whispered close to her ear, "I will never complain when you choose to seek comfort in my embrace."

Elizabeth sniffled loudly.

"Even when I dampen your cravat with my tears?"

He caressed Elizabeth's chin and brushed away the dampness with the pad of his thumb.

"I would suffer that and much more, Elizabeth."

On many planes, Mr. Darcy's deep affection frightened Elizabeth, but today she leaned her head against his chest and closed her eyes. She could smell the sandalwood he used after his morning's ablutions and something very masculine: the essence of him. Foolish as it would sound to those not so romantic as she, it was as if Elizabeth knew his scent and the feel of his fingers tracing a line upon her cheek forever.

Elizabeth did not know how long they sat as such before the sound of horses neighing in the mews behind her uncle's garden brought her to her senses. It bothered Elizabeth to realize how easily Mr. Darcy's act of comfort affected her. With a deep sigh, she straightened her bonnet.

"We should complete our conversation."

"Certainly." He released her, but Elizabeth thought Mr. Darcy did so in reluctance, and that pleased her.

Elizabeth offered him an encouraging smile.

"We should speak of your second offense. Of your relationship with Mr. Wickham."

Mr. Darcy frowned.

Mr. Darcy's Fault

"The tale of Mr. Wickham's lies could prove more problematic."

"How so?"

"If what I shared with you becomes public knowledge, my sister will suffer Society's scorn."

"Miss Darcy?" Elizabeth's voice rose in surprise.

Mr. Darcy's expression darkened in anguish. The pain of what occurred between Darcy and Mr. Wickham lay raw upon the gentleman's features. It was Elizabeth's turn to comfort him; she cupped his larger hand with her two smaller ones. She caressed the back of Mr. Darcy's fist until his palm opened to claim her fingers.

As if he clung to her as a buoy in a sea of despair, Mr. Darcy began his story.

"Mr. Wickham is the son of a very respectful man, who had for many years the management of all the Pemberley estates."

Elizabeth listened in rapt disbelief as Mr. Darcy chronicled the tale of the previous Master of Pemberley's affection for his godson and of Mr. Wickham's betrayal of the late Mr. Darcy's wishes, of Wickham's life of dissipation, and of the man's attempt to elope with Miss Darcy.

"Regard for my sister's credit and feelings prevented any public exposure of Mr. Wickhams' perfidy, but I wrote to Mr. Wickham, who left Ramsgate immediately, and Mrs. Younge was, of course, removed from Georgiana's charge. Mr. Wickham's chief object was, unquestionably, my sister's fortune, which is thirty-thousand pounds, but I cannot help supposing the hope of revenge upon me was a strong inducement." Mr. Darcy added in true wretchedness, "Mr. Wickham's revenge

89

would have been complete indeed."

Listening to Mr. Darcy's explanation, Elizabeth knew astonishment, apprehension, and even horror. She wished to save her pride, to discredit the gentleman's harsh report, but Elizabeth made herself examine the truth of each of Mr. Darcy's assertions. She based her dislike of Mr. Darcy upon his damning treatment of the affable Mr. Wickham; but on closer examination, Mr. Darcy's account of Mr. Wickham's connection with the Pemberley family was exactly what Mr. Wickham related, and the kindness of the late Mr. Darcy, though she did not know before its extent, agreed equally well with Mr. Wickham's own words. However, when it came to the late Mr. Darcy's will, the difference in the tales were glaring.

When Elizabeth thought upon it, she accepted Mr. Wickham's tale because of the man's fine countenance and because Mr. Darcy's refusal to dance with her stung Elizabeth's pride. She knew nothing of what occurred before Darcy's coming to Hertfordshire. As to the real character of both, had information been in her power, Elizabeth never felt a wish of inquiring. Privately, she cursed her insensibility.

How differently did everything now appear: Mr. Wickham's attentions to Miss King were now the consequence of views solely and hatefully mercenary, and his abandonment when learning of the mediocrity of Elizabeth's own fortune proved no longer the moderation of his wishes, but rather Mr. Wickham's eagerness to grasp at anything. At length, Elizabeth saw it all so clearly. With regard to her fortune, Mr. Wickham was either deceived, or he was gratifying his vanity by encouraging the preference, which Elizabeth most incautiously showed.

Mr. Darcy's Fault

Every lingering struggle in Mr. Wickham's favor grew fainter and fainter. If what Mr. Darcy said of Jane and of her family held truth, surely so did his tale of Mr. Wickham. In further justification of Mr. Darcy's character, Elizabeth allowed Mr. Bingley long ago asserted Darcy's blamelessness in the affair.

Elizabeth could no longer account for her previous opinion of Mr. Darcy's manners. The circumstance, which provided her with an intimacy with his ways, proved him to be principled and just. Darcy's connections esteemed and valued him. Even Mr. Wickham allowed Mr. Darcy merit as a brother, and in their earlier interactions Elizabeth often heard Mr. Darcy speak affectionately of his sister. As she listened to Mr. Darcy speak of Georgiana's humiliation, shame filled her.

"Poor Miss Darcy," she whispered into the misery filling the space between them. *No wonder the girl avoided my questions regarding Mr. Wickham.* "We must discover the letter's whereabouts, Mr. Darcy. We cannot permit your sister to know Society's disdain."

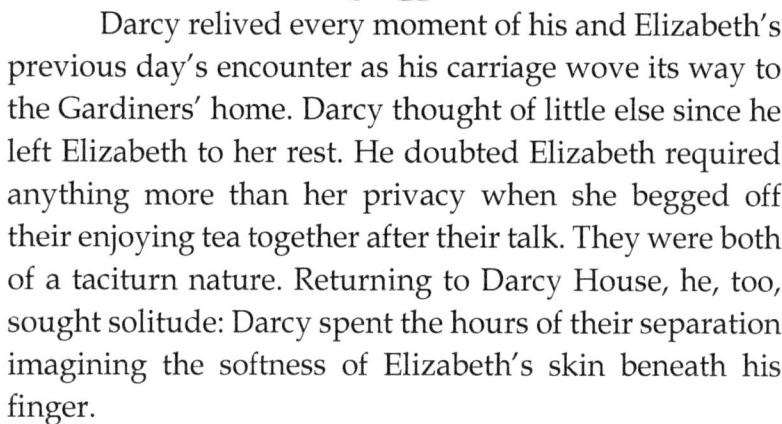

Darcy relived every moment of his and Elizabeth's previous day's encounter as his carriage wove its way to the Gardiners' home. Darcy thought of little else since he left Elizabeth to her rest. He doubted Elizabeth required anything more than her privacy when she begged off their enjoying tea together after their talk. They were both of a taciturn nature. Returning to Darcy House, he, too, sought solitude: Darcy spent the hours of their separation imagining the softness of Elizabeth's skin beneath his finger.

"As silky as I expected," he murmured.

His gaze remained upon the passing scenery, but Darcy's mind sought the exquisite feel of Elizabeth in his embrace. He held her previously, but this time the lady initiated the contact. Elizabeth permitted Darcy to witness the defenselessness of which Mr. Bennet spoke.

"It was a beginning," he whispered.

But her tearful moments of self-recrimination were not the extent of Elizabeth's openness. A smile formed on Darcy's lips as he recalled the other tokens of affection the lady offered. In addition to her stroking of the back of his hand while he spoke of Georgiana's brush with ruination, before Darcy made his exit, Elizabeth rose upon tiptoes, raised her chin, and closed her eyes in preparation for his parting kiss. Her forwardness took him by surprise, but Darcy kept his wits about him. Gathering her once more into his embrace, he kissed Elizabeth with the tenderness of early affections being sowed.

When he entered the Gardiners' front parlor, the memory of the kiss remained, and it was all Darcy could do not to catch her to him and take up where they left off. The welcome of Elizabeth's smile made it more difficult for him to act the gentleman. She extended her hands to him, and Darcy crossed the room to claim them. He kissed the knuckles of first one hand and then the other.

"I am pleased you are looking of health today, my dear."

Elizabeth gestured for him to join her on the settle.

"We are both aware, Mr. Darcy, my pique yesterday came from our conversation."

Darcy waited for Elizabeth to be seated before he claimed the cushion adjoining hers.

"Even so," Darcy said with a grin, "I prefer a bit of

color in your cheeks." He watched as a frown crossed her features and wondered if Elizabeth still held objections to their joining. "Is something amiss? Have I spoken from step?" In the back of his mind the deadline for her decision loomed. Although Elizabeth willingly kissed him, it was possible she might still claim her freedom. How would he go one if the latter proved true?

Elizabeth shook off his question.

"I spent a good portion last evening in self chastisement. It is as if yesterday was the first time I truly saw you."

"I pray you found something you could admire," Darcy ventured.

"Vanity, Mr. Darcy?" Elizabeth cocked an eyebrow in a tease.

Despite his best efforts, blood rushed to Darcy's cheeks.

"A man would like to think the woman he admires finds him worthy of her attentions," Darcy said in his defense.

Elizabeth laughed, and Darcy thought it a magical sound.

"You continue to surprise me, Sir."

"Surprise is better than repulsion." Darcy adopted her lighter tones.

Just for a moment, her hazel eyes darkened, as if she too recalled yesterday's intimacies.

"Yes, I suppose." A coy smile crossed Elizabeth's lips. "I know we have set a new course for our acquaintance several times, but I was wondering if you would consider doing so again? With nothing to merit distrust between us, I would very much like to know how we might get on.

Might we be 'Wills' and 'Lizzy'?"

Darcy surveyed her delicate features. He realized offering him a back door apology cost Elizabeth a bit more of her pride. Sardonic amusement filled his heart.

"*Wills* is it? No one called me such since I was in leading strings."

Elizabeth eyed him with surprise.

"I suspect the endearment came from your mother."

Darcy thought Elizabeth calling him *Wills*, as an endearment, would be most pleasant.

"How did you know?"

Elizabeth's assessing gaze held Elizabeth's.

"You spoke previously of the late Mr. Darcy molding you into Pemberley's master, which is the face you present the world, but of late, I noted qualities not easily observed. I suspect Lady Anne Darcy honed those characteristics she thought would balance your personality. Did not Lady Anne teach *Wills* of empathy and of beauty in nature and of a love of learning?"

"She did."

Darcy tilted his head to the side in examination: Was it possible Elizabeth Bennet's heart softened? Only a few of his most intimate acquaintances ever saw him as anything other than the master of a great estate.

Elizabeth appeared triumphant in her discovery of his other self.

"I am glad to recognize Lady Anne's maternal touch upon you."

Elizabeth's sister entered the room at that exact moment. Darcy suppressed a stab of annoyance with the interruption. A few more moments of privacy might lead to another ready kiss.

"Mr. Bingley has arrived," Miss Bennet announced. "We are to the museum. Would you and Mr. Darcy care to join us?"

Elizabeth shot Darcy an inquiring glance.

"If it is your desire, I am a willing escort," Darcy assured her.

"Yes," Elizabeth announced with a smile of delight. "I wish to become more acquainted with your knowledge of the exhibits, Sir."

Darcy nodded smugly.

"I am up to the challenge, Miss Elizabeth." He paused for emphasis. "By and by, did I neglect to tell you my father's cousin, Samuel Darcy, is one of the major contributors to the museum's display of antiquities? He is a famous archaeologist."

Elizabeth presented Darcy a surprised laugh.

"Did you hear, Jane? Mr. Darcy possesses an extensive knowledge of the displays. We shall be thoroughly entertained."

Miss Bennet eyed Elizabeth closely: obviously, the change in her sister's attitude toward Darcy took Miss Bennet unawares.

"I would expect nothing less of a man of Mr. Darcy's intelligence," Jane Bennet said with a wry twist of her lips. "It will delight our father for you to recount Mr. Darcy's tales when next you write. Mr. Bennet always said you would never settle for a simpleton."

The day at the museum brought Darcy such joy that for a few stolen moments, he abandoned his fear of Georgiana's ruination and his fear of Elizabeth's eventual refusal. A man of more worldly experience than he would likely think Miss Elizabeth's curiosity cumbersome, but Darcy found the lady's insightful questions exhilarating. In the realm of flirtations, Darcy often stumbled. Because of his wealth, women feigned interest in what he shared, but Darcy recognized their true intents written upon their bored expressions. However, Elizabeth Bennet hung on his every observation; she challenged him and teased and was thoroughly enchanting. If his heart were not already engaged, the afternoon's outing would secure Darcy's regard for the woman.

"My father's Cousin Samuel traveled with Alexander von Humboldt in the Americas," Darcy explained as they strolled through the numerous displays. "Naturally, Cousin Samuel's participation piqued my interest in the expeditions. I devoured von Humboldt's earliest accounts of the journey and am anticipating the next volume. Cousin Samuel offered to introduce me to the man if this madness with Napoleon ever knows an end. Von Humboldt took residence in Paris."

"Papa wished to read the gentleman's findings," Elizabeth said with a bit of awe.

Darcy drew her closer for enjoyed the warmth of her body claiming his.

"It would be my pleasure to permit Mr. Bennet to borrow the books. Pemberley's library holds books on a variety of subjects."

Elizabeth glanced at him, and Darcy noted the upcoming tease forming upon her features.

"Do you think to seduce me, Mr. Darcy, with an offer of free rein for my dearest parent in your renowned library?"

Seduce, Darcy thought. *If only.*

"Would my doing so secure your agreement to my proposal, my dear?" Darcy whispered for her ears only.

Elizabeth blushed the most enticing shade of rose.

"I shall add your promise to the list of your positive traits, Sir."

"Is there any chance the positives might some day outweigh the negatives?"

"Perhaps." Elizabeth gifted Darcy with a beguiling smile. "Even your innate stubbornness can be viewed with new eyes."

Darcy barked out a laugh, which had Bingley and Miss Bennet turning to stare back at him.

"You are delightful, Elizabeth Bennet."

Elizabeth tightened her grip upon his elbow.

"Tell me more of Mr. von Humboldt. Papa says the gentleman knows much criticism for his Romantic school of thought and for his neglecting of the human societies of the lower Americas."

The fact Elizabeth Bennet knew something of von Humboldt's studies did not surprise him. In the months Darcy "studied" her, he recognized Elizabeth's potential as the mother of his children. He held no doubt Pemberley's future would depend upon his heir possessing a fine mind for the impossible.

"On the contrary," Darcy explained, "the gentleman dedicated sections of his works upon the poor conditions the African slaves endure each day. Von Humboldt's disgust for the issue of slavery, as well as the inhumane conditions inflicted upon the indigenous peoples by colonial policies coat the man's descriptions. Mr. Bennet would find the gentleman's observations quite informative. As for me, I welcome von Humboldt's observations on guano."

"Guano?" Elizabeth asked with a deepening of her adorable frown lines.

Darcy's lips turned upward.

"It is a type of fertilizer made from the leavings of seabirds, cave bats, and seals. Guano is richer in what the land requires than what we currently use. I instigated a four crop rotation upon the estate, but the land still suffers from overuse. Of late, I invested in an expedition, which will recover guano for importation into England."

"You are always looking to the future," Elizabeth whispered in reverence.

"I hope to secure 'our' future, Miss Elizabeth," Darcy corrected.

Chapter 7

ELIZABETH WATCHED AS MR. DARCY bowed to the attractive brunette flirtatiously twirling her parasol. He returned to his coach to retrieve Elizabeth's parasol, but the woman intercepted him. Elizabeth noted his glance in her direction, but good manners would require Mr. Darcy to be polite to the woman, who boldly caught his hand to drag him a few steps to the left to stand under the shade of a large elm before closing the parasol to stare up at him.

Darcy and Bingley sent notes early to inform her and Jane that they meant to escort "their ladies" to a May Day picnic in Richmond, being hosted by the Countess of Stratown. When they arrived, Elizabeth took such delight in the magnificent greens that she forgot her parasol. Now, she rued her joyful response to being away from the City: The unknown woman stroked Mr. Darcy's arm with her fan, and Elizabeth noted how his shoulders stiffened. It was a stance she observed on multiple occasions, one she misinterpreted as the gentleman's prideful disdain. Now, she knew it nothing more than his societal awkwardness.

Earlier, their foursome feasted upon trout, cold meats, strawberries, hard cheese, dark bread, delicious cakes, and chilled champagne, and Elizabeth enjoyed how the dappled sunlight provided Mr. Darcy a more youthful appearance. He relaxed into a conversation with Bingley regarding textiles and politics, and Elizabeth glimpsed the man of which everyone spoke so fondly. It was the best day of their acquaintance; that is, until the brunette blocked Mr. Darcy's return. Something Elizabeth would not call *jealousy* crept into her chest.

"Who is the lady with Mr. Darcy?" The words slipped out before Elizabeth thought to give voice to her anxiousness.

Mr. Bingley rolled to his side to look in the direction Elizabeth stared.

"Lady Cecilia Longacre." He stretched out again, draping his forearm across his eyes, but Elizabeth noticed the wry twist of Mr. Bingley's lips.

Elizabeth claimed another strawberry to nibble upon its flesh. She would not permit Mr. Bingley's amusement to know of the tightening of her chest. When the woman stroked Mr. Darcy's arm a second time, Elizabeth could bear it no longer.

"Wipe the smile from your lips, Mr. Bingley, and speak to me of Lady Cecilia," Elizabeth said testily.

"As you wish, my dear." Bingley shoved to a seated position. "Lady Cecilia is the second daughter of our host, the Earl of Stratown. His Lordship, James Longacre, is an intimate acquaintance of Darcy's uncle, the Earl of Matlock. The families long thought Darcy and

Lady Cecilia a good match, a fact which once drove my sister Caroline to Bedlam."

"You think I know the green-eyed monster?" Elizabeth accused.

"Your hazel eyes are a bit green today, Lizzy," Jane teased.

Elizabeth ignored her sister's taunt.

"Why would a woman of a titled family choose a mere 'Mister'?" Elizabeth knew instant regret at her loose tongue, but with grace, Mr. Bingley ignored her unintended insult.

"Lady Cecilia is a second daughter, as was Darcy's mother, Lady Anne Fitzwilliam, who married a plain 'mister,'" Bingley chastised. "You forget, Miss Elizabeth, that Darcy's family holds a prominent place in English history. Darcy can trace his roots back to the thirteenth century. The woman he claims to wife will gain more by the connection than a simple title. Lady Cecilia would be pleased to be called *Mrs. Darcy*."

Unknowingly, Elizabeth's frown lines deepened.

"I fear I am quite warm. If Lady Cecilia means to delay Mr. Darcy's return, I must retrieve my parasol from his grasp." She rose quickly: Afraid if Elizabeth thought upon what she would do when she interrupted Mr. Darcy and the woman, she would find fault with her actions. "Pardon me for a moment." Shoulders squared, Elizabeth strode toward where Mr. Darcy conversed with the beautiful Lady Cecilia. Despite her best efforts, Elizabeth grimaced when she heard Bingley's chuckle and Jane's twittering giggle.

As Elizabeth approached the pair, she studied Lady Cecilia's features: Creamy complexion, where freckles from the sun peppered Elizabeth's skin. Silken dark walnut locks, where hers were a drab auburn, a mixture of brown and red and blonde strains–none of them claiming prominence. Tall and slender, much in the form of Miss Bingley, rather than Elizabeth's petite form. Discovering herself wanting, Elizabeth's steps slowed, and she thought to turn away; but Lady Cecilia noted Elizabeth's approach. Mr. Darcy, having read the alarm in his conversation partner's features, turned in Elizabeth's direction. She had no choice but to continue what Elizabeth now realized to be a fool's journey.

"There you are," she said before Mr. Darcy could acknowledge her sudden appearance with a bow of welcome. "I thought my parasol lost, Sir."

Elizabeth's heart raced until the gentleman smiled at her.

"I apologize, my dear," Mr. Darcy said as he offered Elizabeth an elbow, which she gladly claimed. "Lady Cecilia and I were speaking of childhood adventures. I did not mean to inconvenience you."

Despite the smile upon the woman's lips, Lady Cecilia's expression hardened.

"Perhaps, Darcy, you should make me acquainted with your friend." Her gaze slid down Elizabeth's frame, and it was all Elizabeth could do not to blush. Lady Cecilia's day dress was of finest material and her bonnet intricately fashionable. Elizabeth felt quite ashamed of her country appearance.

"Lady Cecilia, may I present Miss Elizabeth Bennet of Longbourn in Hertfordshire." Mr. Darcy flexed his arm muscle to nudge Elizabeth closer, and Elizabeth realized he meant to protect her from Lady Cecilia's barbs. It was the way of Mr. Darcy, placing himself between those he affected and the rest of the world; Elizabeth knew gratitude at engendering his regard.

Elizabeth curtsied.

"Lady Cecilia. I am pleased to take the acquaintance of a long-standing friend of Mr. Darcy's. I apologize for interrupting your reunion. I meant no offense." Elizabeth glanced to the gentleman. "Jane and I thought we might watch the May Day dancers. I required my parasol."

"Permit me to escort you." Mr. Darcy made to offer Lady Cecilia a bow of parting, but the lady stayed his exit.

"You cannot leave so soon, Darcy. I know nothing of Miss Bennet, and you know Stratown will question me upon the acquaintance." Lady Cecilia returned her assessing gaze to Elizabeth. "How long have you and Darcy held a connection?"

Elizabeth understood the woman's unspoken insinuation: Lady Cecilia thought Mr. Darcy fell foul to a country tart who meant to claim his fortune.

"For some nine months," Elizabeth responded in false sweetness.

"That long?" the woman's voice rose in surprise. "Why were we unaware of your time in Hertfordshire, Darcy?"

Elizabeth felt the ripple of contempt moving down Mr. Darcy's frame. His welcoming expression did not change, but the tone of his response spoke of the gentleman's disapproval.

"I am not of the nature, Lady Cecilia, to permit others approval of my business."

The woman ignored Mr. Darcy's warning.

"Nonsense, Darcy. An offense was not my intent.

I just found it odd that Miss Bennet is in London, and we have yet to encounter her at the entertainments. Have you experienced any of the Season, Miss Bennet?'

"I have not, my lady. I arrived in Town only a few weeks prior." Elizabeth came close to mentioning her time at Rosings Park, but she quickly deduced that Lady Catherine informed Lord Matlock of Mr. Darcy's desertion of Miss de Bourgh. Therefore, Lord Stratown likely also knew of Mr. Darcy's participation in Elizabeth's ruination.

"Now, if you will pardon us, my lady," Mr. Darcy said with renewed firmness. "Mr. Bingley and Miss Bennet await our return." He cupped Elizabeth's hand with his free one. With an aristocratic nod of farewell, Mr. Darcy turned Elizabeth's steps in the direction of their blanket upon the mossy ground.

"I apologize," Elizabeth whispered when they were from the earshot of Lady Cecilia.

"Why ever for?" Mr. Darcy asked just as softly.

Elizabeth stepped from his arm. Despite her blinking several times to drive them away, tears misted Elizabeth's eyes.

"Without my participation, I trapped you in a commitment of marriage greatly below your consequence. I falsely assumed we stood upon equal footing: you are a gentleman, and I am a gentleman's daughter, but now I recognize the foolishness of my conceit. My pride permitted me to think even with all her fine manners and schooling, I was a superior choice to Miss Bingley, whose father was part of the trades. Yet, how can I consider myself above the daughter of an earl or even the daughter of a baronet, as is Miss de Bourgh? No one outside my family circle knows of our arrangement, Mr. Darcy. Uncle Gardiner has relatives in Edinburgh, and Uncle assures me I can live with them until the scandal subsides. If you wish it, I will release you from our bargain." Elizabeth's bottom lip trembled with trepidation.

Mr. Darcy closed the distance between them.

"If Society permitted me to do so, I would clasp you to me and kiss away your fears," Mr. Darcy said upon a breathy whisper. "Please look at me, Elizabeth."

His words brought the tears closer to spilling over, but Elizabeth did as the gentleman requested. Mr. Darcy's countenance, so familiar now, was the dearest upon which Elizabeth ever looked.

"The only way you are going to Edinburgh is in my traveling coach, and we will stop in Gretna Green and speak our vows over the anvil. If you leave so as to protect me, I will follow and claim your affections upon Scottish soil. However, if your heart lies elsewhere..."

"It does not, Sir," Elizabeth said quickly to assure him of her growing devotion.

"Then we will spend the last week of our arrangement as we have done of late. We will discover more of each other to admire. At the end, you will speak your heart, and I will speak mine."

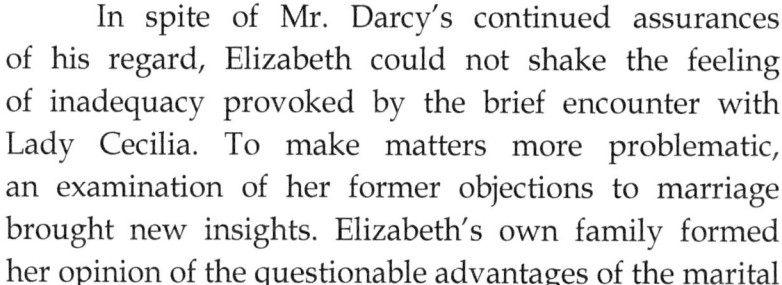

In spite of Mr. Darcy's continued assurances of his regard, Elizabeth could not shake the feeling of inadequacy provoked by the brief encounter with Lady Cecilia. To make matters more problematic, an examination of her former objections to marriage brought new insights. Elizabeth's own family formed her opinion of the questionable advantages of the marital arrangement. Needless to say, her parents' marriage did not show a very pleasing picture of conjugal felicity or domestic comfort.

Her father, captivated by youth and beauty, and that appearance of good humor which youth and beauty give, married a woman whose weak understanding and illiberal mind, had very early in their marriage, put an end to all real affection for her. Respect, esteem, and confidence vanished forever, and all her father's views of domestic happiness dissipated.

The only saving grace of the situation Elizabeth could name was the state of her father's disposition. Unlike other men who would seek "comfort' for the disappointment which his marriage engendered, her father found his enjoyments in his country estate and in his books. To her mother, Mr. Bennet was little otherwise indebted than as her ignorance and folly contributed to his amusement. In hindsight, Elizabeth saw her father's cynical nature as not the sort of happiness either a man would, in general, wish to owe to his wife or as a model she should emulate.

Although Elizabeth never knew blindness in regard to the impropriety of her father's behavior as a husband, she always viewed Mr. Bennet's disdain with pain; but, respecting his quick mind and grateful for his affectionate treatment of her, Elizabeth endeavored to forget what she could not overlook, and to banish from her thoughts that continual breach of conjugal obligation of decorum which, in exposing his wife to the contempt of her children, proved so highly reprehensible. But Elizabeth never felt so strongly as now the disadvantages, which must attend the children of so unsuitable a marriage.

"But Mr. Darcy is not of the same nature as is Papa," Elizabeth told her reflection in the window glass. "And I am nothing of Mama's disposition. Yet, even so, is there any reason we should marry?" She squeezed into the small window box seat to stare out at the darkness. "You enjoy the gentleman's company." Elizabeth thought to enumerate the reasons for their joining, as well as those against. "He is accepting of your opinions and treats you with more respect than would most gentlemen. You both enjoy the country, but I would admit to requiring a bit more of Society than does Mr. Darcy." Elizabeth expelled a pleased chuckle. "Perhaps, Mr. Darcy would not appear so from sorts if he accompanied me to the entertainments." They attended several musicals and plays of late. "These past weeks, Mr. Darcy appeared more comfortable when we were in public. He laughed at the comedy last evening and is always sociable with familiar company."

Elizabeth ticked off Mr. Darcy's assets upon her fingers.

"I would also admit to knowing regret when Mr. Darcy has other obligations and does not call." Until now, Elizabeth gave little thought beyond their immediate future; however, she realized her customary need to keep the gentleman at a distance transformed to a need for his closeness. The thought of Mr. Darcy's kisses brought warmth to her heart and created a yearning Elizabeth could not explain.

Without thinking, she squirmed and fanned her cheeks with her hands.

"How bizarre," Elizabeth chastised, but a second flush of color had her analyzing her reaction. "Have I developed a *tendre* for the man?" In the past, a severe frown would announce Elizabeth's disapproval of such random thoughts. Instead, a devilish grin claimed her lips. "I believe I have," she declared. "My!" Elizabeth giggled in shameful joy. "Would Mr. Darcy not know surprise with that particular fact?" Well able to imagine the gentleman's shock when she announced the arrival of her affections, Elizabeth laughed aloud. "I must tell him. Mr. Darcy deserves to know my heart is equally engaged as is his."

"Mr. Darcy." Elizabeth welcomed him with a smile before extending her hands in Mr. Darcy's direction.

Following a quick bow, Darcy crossed the room to catch her hands in his.

"You hold no idea how often I desired such a greeting upon your lips," he whispered as he bent to brush a kiss across her upturned cheek. "Tell me what brings such joy to your eyes."

"Nothing of note," Elizabeth said as she gestured him to a place beside her upon the settle. "Why do you not speak of your day? I am certain it was more important than mine, which was marked by a continuation of my poor needlework, much to my aunt's chagrin."

The gentleman chuckled.

"You will be pleased to know at Pemberley there are several maids to see to the mending."

"Bless you, Sir," Elizabeth said with an exaggerated dip of her head. "I fear I am a lost cause."

"I am at your service?" Mr. Darcy smiled, and Elizabeth's heart did a double flip. His was an expressive smile, and Elizabeth wondered for a moment how Mr. Darcy ever learned to school his expressions. He caught her hand, and again the warmth of her newfound feelings filled her. "I cannot say my day did not know its trials, but I will not claim those obstacles more important than your mending Mr. Gardiners' stockings."

Elizabeth's smile widened.

"Aunt Gardiner would never trust me with Uncle Edward's stockings." She interlaced their fingers. "What trials did you encounter today?"

Mr. Darcy tilted his head in a familiar manner.

"An estate as large as Pemberley requires constant supervision. I placed an order for the construction of a new mill to serve my cottagers at Pemberley, as well as a forge at my mother's property in Somersetshire."

"I was unaware of the Somersetshire property."

The gentleman presented her a small shrug of acceptance.

"The property came under my father's care as part of Lady Anne's dowry. Since coming into my father's position, I made extensive repairs to the manor house and the land. Depending on whom Georgiana chooses to husband, I may consider it as part of her dowry. A second son, for example, would require property to establish a home for my sister. I do not wish formally to include the estate in Georgiana's dowry for it would tempt less honorable suitors."

"Such as Mr. Wickham, " Elizabeth reasoned aloud.

"As godson to my late father, Mr. Wickham was privy to information regarding the sums placed aside for Georgiana's dowry. I never announced my sister's wealth for it would turn her into a 'desired morsel' by unscrupulous rogues. I will not have Georgiana's name upon the lips of Society's scoundrels."

Elizabeth studied Mr. Darcy's countenance: The depth of the gentleman's loyalty no longer surprised her.

"If not part of Miss Darcy's dowry, one of your own children could inherit the property." Elizabeth found herself blushing when Mr. Darcy's eyes darkened.

"Yours is a lovely thought," he whispered. Elizabeth knew his mind drifted to her begetting those said children, but surprisingly, the idea no longer held revulsion.

After an elongated pause, she cleared her throat.

"Are there other properties?" It would not do for them to dwell on images of marital intimacies.

"A hunting lodge in Lincolnshire and a large farm in Warwickshire."

Elizabeth could feel Mr. Darcy's pulse quicken as he looked upon her. It was quite disconcerting, as well as exhilarating at the same time.

"What shall we do this afternoon?" she asked upon a breathy exhale.

Mr. Darcy leaned closer to steal a quick kiss.

"I hoped you would join me in the purchase of a gift for Georgiana's birthday."

A grin of surprise claimed Elizabeth's lips.

"When is Miss Darcy's birthday?"

"Not for two months, but I plan a special gift, which will take time to assemble and deliver. Will you accompany me? I would treasure your opinions."

"You shall rue the day you sought my opinions, Mr. Darcy," Elizabeth said in jest.

He lifted Elizabeth's fingers to his lips and gave them a loving nuzzle. Elizabeth discovered a warmth spread through her veins.

"I will have no peace until you rule my life, Elizabeth Bennet."

Chapter 8

THE EARLY AFTERNOON proved itself spectacular, one in which Elizabeth saw her blossoming affections for Mr. Darcy take a giant leap forward. He escorted Elizabeth to a shop near her uncle's home.

"I noted the store front before the warehouse when I called upon you last week," Mr. Darcy explained. "I since spoke to the proprietor regarding my purchase. Yet, before I confirm the order, I seek your opinion on whether my proposed gift will please my sister."

"My acquaintance with Miss Darcy is of such short duration," Elizabeth protested.

"But you understand the tastes of girls fresh from the schoolroom," Mr. Darcy countered.

And so, Elizabeth assisted Mr. Darcy in the purchase of a petite pianoforte, one designed to fit into the sitting room of Miss Darcy's private quarters.

"There is a larger instrument in Pemberley's music room, but I thought Georgiana could have use of the smaller one when she marries and leaves home."

Elizabeth glanced up at him.

"The smaller instrument would also suit the manor house in Somersetshire?'

"It would," Mr. Darcy admitted.

Elizabeth gave her head a shake of disbelief.

"You always plan for the unseen, Mr. Darcy. I would dislike being your opponent in a game of strategy. The rumors of your quick intelligence did not speak of this facet of your personality."

The gentleman frowned.

"Do you find my need to prepare for all possibilities cumbersome?"

"Lord, no," Elizabeth declared as she wrapped her gloved hands about his elbow. "I am simply grateful you placed me among those you affect."

Mr. Darcy leaned closer to speak to Elizabeth's ears only.

"I would place Pemberley's fortune and my devotion at your feet."

For a moment, Elizabeth thought he might kiss her, even though they stood in the center of Mr. Watson's Music Emporium. At length, Mr. Darcy caught her hand.

"Come, my dear. You must play for me." Mr. Darcy directed Elizabeth toward a lovely pianoforte, one whose case displayed intricate carvings of angels.

"Mr. Darcy..." Elizabeth tugged at his hand. "You know my fingers refuse to obey even my simplest command. I would prefer not to embarrass you with my poor showing."

Mr. Darcy pulled her close.

"Play for me, Elizabeth." The gentleman coaxed

on a breathy exhale. "At Lucas Lodge, you played for the entertainment of Sir William's guests. At Rosings, my cousin knew your favor. I wish to hear you play for *me*. I promise to find no fault."

Mr. Darcy seated her at one of Mr. Watson's instruments, and Elizabeth played while Mr. Darcy sat close beside her to turn the pages. The moment knew a sprinkle of magic: Mr. Darcy's presence warmed her heart, and Elizabeth played for him. His breath caressed her cheek, and love swelled to claim her breathing. Elizabeth never played so well: The moment intimate and filling. The hollow of loneliness swelled over with her newfound affections.

"That was magnificent," Mr. Darcy whispered when no more notes remained. "It was as perfect as I imagined."

Unfortunately, the magic dissipated when they returned to her uncle's house.

"Ah, Mr. Darcy," Uncle Edward called as they entered the house. "I am pleased you arrived before I returned to my office to finish out the day."

Mr. Darcy assisted Elizabeth with her wrap.

"May I be of service, Mr. Gardiner?"

"Yes, you may," Uncle Gardiner declared. "The gentleman from Germany of which we spoke last week arrived in London, and he insists Mrs. Gardiner and I join him at Vauxhall Gardens this evening for supper. I hoped you and Mr. Bingley could escort my nieces. Herr Herriman demands much of my attention, and I would feel better if you and Mr. Bingley were close to protect Miss Bennet and Elizabeth."

Mr. Darcy stiffened, and Elizabeth recognized his

immediate disapproval.

"I have a prior engagement with my uncle, the Earl of Matlock," Mr. Darcy said in apology. "I fear my uncle would find my absence most inconvenient." Elizabeth understood Mr. Darcy's unspoken explanation. The earl summoned Darcy to defend Elizabeth's presence in the gentleman's life.

Uncle Gardiner nodded his disappointment.

"I suppose Mr. Bingley is up to snuff. He may tend both Jane and Lizzy."

"I do not understand, Sir. Why is it necessary for Miss Bennet and Miss Elizabeth to attend a supper designed for business? Vauxhall is not for the faint of heart." Mr. Darcy turned to her. "I know it is beyond the limits of our connection, but I would prefer you did not attend the entertainments tonight."

Although Mr. Darcy's words did not surprise her, Elizabeth found her ire rising.

"You would have me sit at home while both you and uncle's households enjoy the evening," she accused.

"Vauxhall's reputation is well earned," Mr. Darcy countered. "It is not safe for an unescorted lady."

Elizabeth knew Mr. Darcy meant well–knew she over reacted–knew she could be sabotaging the joy she knew of late, but Elizabeth could not stifle her demand for independence. Even though Elizabeth would not admit it to herself, her feared an illusion of happiness. *Was it not better to live alone than to live under any man's rule?*

"I have yet to accept your proposal, Sir," she snapped. "However, you presume to exact your will over my comings and goings."

Elizabeth held no great desire to experience

Vauxhall's pleasures, especially without Mr. Darcy at her side, but she would not permit any man to subjugate her: She would not be Mr. Darcy's chattel.

"Now, if you will pardon me, I must dress for the evening. Uncle will show you out." Without looking back at him, she started for the stairs. At the landing, Elizabeth paused to speak to Mr. Darcy. "Perhaps it is best, Sir, if you no longer call upon me. When you meet with Lord Matlock this evening, inform the earl that the lady ended your connection. I am certain the information will please His Lordship."

As she rushed to her quarters, Elizabeth heard her uncle and Mr. Darcy plead for her return, but she could not think about her rashness without misery claiming her.

Darcy departed the Gardiners' Town house, with assurances from Elizabeth's aunt and uncle that they would speak to their niece regarding her hasty remarks. It was all Darcy could do not to storm the steps to Elizabeth's room, but he could not continue cocking a snook at propriety.

"Elizabeth is simply frightened by her change in her feelings for you," Mrs. Gardiner reasoned, but Darcy questioned whether Elizabeth meant to provide him hope and then destroy him.

The lady has long claimed to despise me. The thought beat out a tattoo in Darcy's brain until he could think of little else, and so when his Uncle Matlock confronted Darcy regarding Elizabeth's lack of connections, Darcy lost his desire to respond with his customary respect for his late mother's only brother.

"Whom I choose to wife is none of your concern,

Sir," he snapped.

"Darcy!" his aunt warned in aghast.

"I apologize, Aunt, but I must act in a manner that will benefit my estate and the future of Pemberley. I do not require a large dowry to keep Pemberley solid; I require a woman to stand beside me in my mission."

His Aunt Nora's eyebrow rose in cynicism.

"And you believe Miss Elizabeth will fill that role with merit?"

If the countess asked the same question only a day prior, Darcy would answer with a resounding affirmation. Today, he held his doubts as to whether Elizabeth would accept him, but not his need for the woman.

"I do."

With a flick of her wrist, the countess interrupted her husband's objection.

"Fitzwilliam explained what occurred at Rosings; the colonel says you proposed to the lady prior to her accident."

Darcy thought it ironic that none of his dear relatives considered the possibility of Elizabeth's refusal.

"I did."

"Then it is as it should be," his Aunt Nora declared. "Matlock promised your father he would continue to guide your steps as Pemberley's master, but long before George Darcy's passing, I promised Lady Anne that I would stand against those who would deny you happiness. If Miss Elizabeth is the choice of your heart, you have my blessing."

With a smile plastered upon her lips, Elizabeth followed her uncle and the German businessman Mr.

Gardiner courted through the crowd swarming Vauxhall's well-lit walkways. She never imagined such grandeur; yet, even so, none of it brought Elizabeth joy.

"Herr Herriman has let a box for the evening and ordered our supper. Likely, we will dine on some form of sauerbraten or wurst." Aunt Gardiner spoke tongue-in-cheek. "I asked cook to leave out something more palpable," her aunt whispered in amusement.

"We shall make the best of whatever the gentleman chose," Elizabeth assured with a giggle. "Although as for me, I would enjoy a taste of the famous rote grutze." Elizabeth glanced to where Mr. Gardiner and the German gentleman waited for them. "I mean to prove uncle proud."

"Even though your heart is breaking?" her aunt probed.

Elizabeth would like to deny how she regretted her actions the moment the door to her quarters closed behind her, but she could not: Elizabeth missed Mr. Darcy at her side.

"Even though."

"Do not fret," Mrs. Gardiner cautioned. "Mr. Darcy will not desert you. The gentleman will call tomorrow, and you may both speak your apologies. Now, come along. Your uncle is motioning us to join him."

Elizabeth swallowed her tears. She prayed her aunt had the right of it for, otherwise, she would shame herself by begging for the man's forgiveness upon the threshold of Darcy House.

The colonel joined his parents for supper, and Darcy's cousin soothed the earl's feathers with tales of

Miss Elizabeth's fending off Lady Catherine's barbs.

"Must be a quick witted chit," His Lordship observed between courses. "Not many can turn my sister's sharp tongue to honey."

The colonel laughed.

"The lady managed to thwart my imperious aunt, her bungling cousin, Mr. Collins, who is Lady Catherine's new cleric, and Darcy. I enjoyed the entertainment. If I did not see it for myself, I would never believe the spectacle."

Aunt Nora turned to Darcy.

"Is the lady only accepting your plight because of your assistance during her accident. Does not Miss Elizabeth return your regard?"

Darcy froze, his fork held in suspension. *Should I admit the truth behind my aunt's accusation?*

Before Darcy could respond, the colonel snatched the lie from his lips.

"Miss Elizabeth is as much besotted with Darcy as he is with her. Admittedly, on first taking the lady's acquaintance, I thought her less than enchanted with Darcy, but one only needs to hear them verbally spar to recognize the true respect they hold for each other. And it is quite apparent Miss Elizabeth is not impressed with Darcy's wealth: The lady made no show to impress Darcy, even though the match would be a brilliant one for her."

"I should explain," Darcy said in earnest. "On our first acquaintance, I made an ill remark about the poor company found at the Meryton's assembly, and Miss Elizabeth overheard my disdain. The lady took offense of my words, and it was necessary for me to prove myself before she would accept me." He chuckled in remembrance. "In truth, Miss Elizabeth's initial indifference drew me to her."

The colonel's lips turned up in a wide grin.

"Perhaps Society mamas should take a page from Miss Elizabeth's book. Mayhap then, more men would seek the parson's noose."

After supper, Darcy made his excuses. All the talk of Elizabeth increased his heart's longing for her.

"Vauxhall," he instructed his coachman.

Inside his carriage's shadows, Darcy planned how he would search out Elizabeth among the pleasure garden's partygoers and would beg her forgiveness before pulling her into the garden's darker paths to steal a kiss or two to seal their joining. He would not permit a moment of pique to ruin their chances at happiness.

"Miss Elizabeth." She looked up at the sound of a masculine voice calling her name with the hope that Mr. Darcy had come at last, only to find the gentleman's long-time nemesis striding in her direction.

"What is Mr. Wickham doing here?" Bingley asked under his breath.

Elizabeth noted the look of disapproval crossing Mr. Bingley's features.

"I do not know," Elizabeth hissed from the corner of her mouth, "but for once this evening I am grateful for Mr. Darcy's absence."

"Imagine encountering you in London," Mr. Wickham said with an amiable smile. "Mr. Bingley. Miss Bennet." Mr. Wickham bowed to her family. "How fortuitous to renew our acquaintance."

Jane and Bingley returned Wickham's bow of greeting, but Elizabeth did not: Her loyalties rested with

Mr. Darcy, and the man before her, no matter how fine his countenance, betrayed his childhood friend.

"We meant to watch the fireworks before returning to my uncle's box," Elizabeth said with dismissive curtness.

Yet, the gentleman ignored her tone.

"Then I will join you if I may? I came to Vauxhall specifically for the fireworks." He offered Jane his elbow, and Elizabeth noted her sister's reluctance in accepting Mr. Wickham's arm.

"We must be rid of him," Mr. Bingley demanded in a harsh whisper as he and Elizabeth fell in behind Wickham and Jane. "If Darcy were to learn I permitted the man to join us, I will lose Darcy's support of my latest business venture."

It did not surprise Elizabeth that Mr. Darcy extended his benevolence to Mr. Bingley, but it did surprise her that Bingley feared Darcy's abandonment.

"I shall speak to Mr. Wickham and explain my understanding with Mr. Darcy. Then I shall send him on his way. Mr. Darcy need not be the wiser."

Mr. Bingley nodded his agreement, and so when they reached the point where Jane and Mr. Wickham awaited them, Bingley reclaimed Jane's hand. The pair stepped closer to the display while Elizabeth removed from the path to permit others to pass.

"I was unaware you were in London or I would have called upon you." Just for a moment, Elizabeth thought she read something "dark" in the gentleman's eyes, but the instant passed too quickly for her to assess what Mr. Wickham's unspoken expression carried.

"From the last correspondence from my sisters, I

thought you in Meryton," Elizabeth said testily. "What of the militia?"

"Colonel Forester sends regular correspondence to his superiors. Captain Denny and I assumed the duties of courier."

A frown caught Elizabeth's nose.

"I cannot imagine Colonel Forester would approve of your spending time at Vauxhall if your assignment was one of messenger."

"The colonel's work is complete for this day, and I am permitted a personal life beyond my duties to the militia." Mr. Wickham presented a warm smile. " "I understand you traveled to Kent."

"Who would speak of my parting?" Elizabeth demanded.

"I regularly dine with Meryton's residents. Much is said of your and Miss Lucas's time with the Collinses."

Although she knew the possibility existed of Maria Lucas's carrying the tale of Elizabeth's engagement to Hertfordshire, Elizabeth hoped Miss Lucas would act more prudently. After all, Mr. Darcy explained to her how he spoke to Elizabeth's father on the best way to approach Sir William regarding Maria's keeping the news private until an official announcement was made.

"Then you must also hold knowledge of Mr. Darcy's presence in Kent."

Mr. Wickham looked surprised, displeased, alarmed, but with a moment's recollection, a smile returned to his lips.

"I was." He looked toward the mingling crowd. "Did my former friend show better than he did in Hertfordshire?"

"Mr. Darcy's manners improve upon acquaintance." Elizabeth spoke in calm, direct tones.

"Indeed!" cried Mr. Wickham, with a flicker of contempt in his voice. "And pray, may I ask—" but checking himself, he added in a gayer tone: "Is it in address that Mr. Darcy improves? Did he deign to add aught of civility to his ordinary style? For I dare not hope," Mr. Wickham continued, in a lower and more serious tone, "that Darcy improved in essentials."

"Oh, no!" said Elizabeth, "in essentials, I believe, Mr. Darcy is very much what he ever was." Mr. Wickham listened with what appeared to be apprehension, as well as anxious attention, a fact that surprised her, but Elizabeth continued her explanation. She could not help but wonder what deceit Mr. Wickham practiced. If Wickham knew Elizabeth traveled to Kent, did the gentleman also know of Elizabeth's impending betrothal? Elizabeth wished she addressed this facet of her understanding with Mr. Darcy to her father; then she would be better armed to handle Mr. Wickham's curiosity.

"When I said Mr. Darcy improved on acquaintance," she continued guardedly, "I did not mean that either Mr. Darcy's mind or manners know improvement; but from knowing him better Mr. Darcy's disposition is more fully understood. Although what I share is not yet common knowledge, I should warn you Mr. Darcy and I hold an understanding. The banns will be called soon. Mr. Darcy apprised me of what occurred between you. Under the circumstances, I think it best if we once again part in good humor." She curtsied. "Now if you will pardon me, I should rejoin Jane and Mr. Bingley."

"Not so quickly, Miss Elizabeth," Wickham

Mr. Darcy's Fault

shushed. He caught Elizabeth's arm and held her in place.

Darcy gave the booth where the Gardiners and Mr. Herriman spoke congenially a wide berth. When he realized neither Elizabeth nor Miss Bennet attended their aunt, Darcy avoided Elizabeth's relations. He would make his apologies later; for now, all he wanted was to look upon Elizabeth's sweet countenance. Even is she were still angry with him, being able to speak to her–to reason with her–would be infinitely better than their separation.

Darcy turned his steps toward the area where the fireworks display would take place. If Elizabeth were among those enjoying the gardens, her curiosity would draw her toward the "show." Darcy paused briefly to look upon those enjoying the orchestra. *His* Elizabeth loved to dance and to socialize. As much as he wished to have her at Pemberley and purely to himself, Darcy made a silent commitment not to permit his selfish need for the woman to smother the delight he found in her.

Not finding Elizabeth among those partaking of the music, Darcy moved on. He kept his gaze upon the open area ahead. Even though Darcy recognized several among the crowd, he pretended not to note their gestures of greeting. Once Elizabeth returned to his side, he would seek out old acquaintances to introduce her.

At length, he reached the area where the crowd thickened. Turning slowly in a circle, Darcy scanned the partygoers for the one countenance, which would ease his anxiety. He spotted a couple near the front he thought to be Bingley and Miss Bennet, but Elizabeth was not at her sister's side. *Had Elizabeth remained at home as he asked?*

"Surely Elizabeth would not wander off alone. Not

in such a dangerous place," Darcy murmured.

Then his eye fell upon a familiar figure: in fact, two familiar figures. Mr. Wickham escorted Elizabeth into the dark mazes surrounding the garden's well-lit promenade.

"No doubt an assignation." Darcy's lips formed the words, but no sound came forth. Someone must have struck him in the chest for Darcy could not breathe. He would like to look down to tend his injury, but his eyes would not remove from the spot he last saw Elizabeth. *She did not fight Wickham,* Darcy's mind announced. *Elizabeth wishes to continue her relationship with Mr. Wickham. Your hopes will know no fruition. Your fault for expecting a different outcome.*

With more sadness than he thought he could bear, Darcy retreated to the parallel paths. He wished no one to know of his awareness of Elizabeth Bennet's betrayal. There would be time enough for his family and friends to express their all-knowing words of consolation.

Chapter 9

"YOU WILL RELEASE ME," Elizabeth ordered as Mr. Wickham pulled her deeper into the darkness.

"In a moment," he growled as Wickham's grip tightened upon Elizabeth's arm. He jerked her hard against his side. Half lifting Elizabeth from the ground Wickham dragged her through the narrow opening in the hedges. She thought to fight him, but the hedges slapped Elizabeth in the face when she turned to strike Mr. Wickham's arm.

"This will do," he snapped. His quick halt sent Elizabeth slamming into his side and knocked the breath from her.

"Do for what?" she rasped. It was all Elizabeth could do to breathe, but she possessed the good sense to keep her mind about her. Despite Mr. Wickham's rough handling of her person, she did not fear the man; rather, she feared what Mr. Darcy would do when he learned of his former friend's boldness. Mr. Darcy's honor would demand he call out Mr. Wickham, and win or lose, Mr. Darcy would forfeit his good name, and it would be her fault for his downfall. "Say what you mean to say and then leave me be."

Mr. Wickham stepped away from her. He stood looking off in the direction of the distant lights of the garden's walkway.

"How do you know I do not plan a seduction?" Bitterness marked his tone. "I am certain Darcy warned you I often act the role of scoundrel."

Her breath returned, and Elizabeth straightened her shoulders.

"You cannot seduce the unwilling," she declared with baldness. "And as to your accusation, Mr. Darcy speaks only of the grief of losing a cherished friend."

Wickham chuckled, but Elizabeth sensed irony in his tone when he spoke.

"You would soften Darcy's many faults."

"And the gentleman shall soften mine." Elizabeth never knew more certainty in her words: She and Mr. Darcy would serve each other well.

Mr. Wickham sighed with resignation.

"I fear not, Miss Elizabeth, for I mean to claim you to wife."

Elizabeth glanced about her. Although life brimmed within Vauxhall's thoroughfare, not even a rabbit was to be found where she stood.

"If you mean to bring ruin to my name, know I shall fight you, Mr. Wickham." She braced her stance for his advance.

"No, you will not." He shook his head in denial. "You will come to me because it will be the only means to

Mr. Darcy's Fault

spare your precious Darcy from public shame."

"I do not understand.'

Mr. Wickham donned his customary air of casual familiarity.

"Then I will explain it all." He caught one of the branches requiring trimming and plunked several leaves from the stem as he spoke. "Some four weeks prior, Colonel Forester sent me on an errand to deliver a message to his counterparts in Kent. The assignment delighted me for I learned you were a guest of Mrs. Collins, and I thought to call upon you."

"You mean I was a guest upon the estate of Mr. Darcy's aunt?" Elizabeth accused. "Did you think Lady Catherine would offer you a place at her table?"

Mr. Wickham eyed Elizabeth in a meaningful fashion.

"I would never aspire to such grandeur," he said in bitterness. "I am too far removed from Her Ladyship's vision to think Lady Catherine de Bourgh would consent to my presence in her drawing room."

"But I never encountered you in the neighborhood." Elizabeth's mind raced to discover Mr. Wickham's duplicity. "Did you change your plans once you learned of Mr. Darcy's presence at Rosings Park?"

Mr. Wickham smiled with sardonic amusement, and Elizabeth experience a shiver of dread shooting down her spine.

"No. It seems I arrived on the very day of your accident." He edged closer, and it was all Elizabeth could do not to retreat. "You were quite distressed as you strode through Rosings' parkland."

"You were in the woods!" she charged. "The dogs.

129

I heard them barking before I fell."

"Yes. They were most insistent. I believe the animals thought I marked you as my prey," Mr. Wickham admitted. "Scampering up a tree not only provided me an escape, but also a bird's eye view of the woods."

"Then you witnessed my accident. Why did you not lend your assistance?" His actions puzzled Elizabeth.

Mr. Wickham stared off in the distance once again. Elizabeth wished she could see what he did. Perhaps then she could find a means from whatever the gentleman planned.

"The hounds meant to protect you," he said at length. "Do you not recall how the blood laid down beside you?"

"Mr. Darcy did not fear the dogs," Elizabeth said a bit too quickly.

Mr. Wickham merely smiled at her blunt allegation.

"You are correct. The very honorable Darcy won over the animals and rescued the damsel. Very righteous of my long time chum."

Elizabeth once termed Mr. Darcy's response to her vulnerability as "highhandedness." Now, she would give anything to have the man come to her rescue.

"If you observed Mr. Darcy's heroics," Elizabeth reasoned. "You are aware his actions compromised my reputation. We agreed to marry."

For the first time since the day she cursed Mr. Darcy's letter, Elizabeth knew marrying Mr. Darcy was her fondest wish.

Mr. Wickham did not bother to disguise his displeasure.

"Oh, yes, Darcy quite thoroughly compromised

you, but I also observed how he did not regret losing his bachelorhood to you. Miss Lucas shared the happy tidings of your impending engagement with me when I called upon Hunsford Cottage on the day Darcy sent you to Town. Your cousin knew less pleasure in your joining, as is correct when Mr. Collins must depend on Lady Catherine's goodwill, but Miss Maria held high hopes for the match."

Elizabeth recognized how Mr. Wickham acted with calculated calmness; however, she had yet to understand his full intent.

"If you spoke to Maria Lucas, then you realize Mr. Darcy and I must marry. The girl will carry her tale of my ruin to Meryton, and the gossips will destroy my other sisters' chances to find a match."

Mr. Wickham's fingers lifted Elizabeth's chin.

"I realize you must marry," he corrected. "But Darcy is not your only choice of husbands."

A stab of exasperation claimed Elizabeth's response.

"Why would I choose another?"

Wickham gave Elizabeth's nose a bit of a buss.

"Because I am in possession of a detailed account of Mr. Darcy's disdain for your family, as well as Miss Darcy's brush with love, and I possess a friend who promised to return my gaming vows if I permit him to print the text in his weekly newsprint. In addition to increasing his readership, it seems my new acquaintance holds no affection for 'His Holiness.' The two often butted heads while at university. He and I would both enjoy seeing Darcy brought low."

"The letter," Elizabeth whispered. "Mr. Darcy's

letter." An unfamiliar flare of doom filled her chest.

"Yes. The noble Darcy left it behind. You see he held no true regard for your safety. My former friend freed you from the trapper's lure only to deliver you into my hands. Your future comes in a package tied with the strings created from Mr. Darcy's faults."

Elizabeth attempted to conceal her panic.

"Mr. Darcy will pay you for the return of the letter."

Frost coated Mr. Wickham's words.

"I have no doubt Darcy will be generous 'to a fault,' so to say. My old friend will know regret for denying me the Klympton living."

"Permit me to speak to Mr. Darcy in your behalf," Elizabeth acknowledge wryly. "Mr. Darcy will listen to me in this matter."

Mr. Wickham frowned in a manner, which proved the gentleman distracted.

"I fear, my dear, you do not comprehend. I will sell the letter to Darcy for a sizeable contribution to my purse, but I also mean to claim you as wife. As such, I will not have you plead for Darcy's benevolence."

"Why?" Elizabeth shook her head in disbelief. "You hold no care for me."

Mr. Wickham appeared offended by her remark.

"Not true. We were once quite taken with each other, and I must admit if you can bring the great Fitzwilliam Darcy to his knees, I am intrigued by the possibilities of what you might exact upon a mere mortal, such as I."

"What if I refuse?" Elizabeth ventured.

Mr. Wickham drawled in ugly tones.

"My offer is not one or the other: If you refuse hand, then I turn the letter over to my new friend. I wis. both Darcy's funds and the woman he means to claim to wife." Mr. Wickham's expression retreated behind a mask of cold civility. "Just think of Darcy's anguish when he views you heavy with my child. It will be a turn of the knife in his gut."

Wickham returned her to where Jane and Bingley waited, but not before Mr. Wickham instructed Elizabeth into how she was to approach Mr. Darcy.

"Early tomorrow you will send Darcy a note to apprise him of my demands. Five thousand pounds: One to settle my debts and another four as payment for my refusal of the Klympton living. Tell Darcy you will serve as my courier. You should also inform the gentleman of your change in allegiance."

"I will not!" Elizabeth declared. "If you wish to negotiate with Mr. Darcy, you will do so without my involvement."

Wickham's features stiffened with irritation.

"Meaning you wish to retain Mr. Darcy's goodwill."

Tears misted Elizabeth's eyes.

"My becoming Mrs. Wickham will be betrayal enough at my hands."

Wickham glared at Elizabeth in open disapproval, but at length, he conceded.

"Very well." He caught her fingers to brush a kiss across Elizabeth's knuckles. "I will come for you tomorrow at midnight. I will be waiting in the mews behind your uncle's house. Do not fail me. Miss Bennet's future and that of your sisters in Hertfordshire depend upon your obedience. You spoke earlier of how difficult it would be for the Bennet daughters to find a husband if you did not marry Mr. Darcy. Just think how public knowledge of Mr. Darcy's letter would compound their woes. And what of poor Georgiana? Miss Darcy will possess no future, even if her dowry is a temptation. She will be sold to a man who would marry the devil for her thirty thousand pounds."

Then Wickham left her as Jane and Bingley approached. Elizabeth had no idea whether her responses to their inquiries as to whether she enjoyed the light show made any sense. All Elizabeth could think upon was the enormity of her loss. Jane's countenance glowed with happiness. Could Elizabeth selfishly snatch away her favorite sister's future in order to claim her own? And why would Mr. Darcy still desire her agreement if his connection to her brought public humiliation to his door and ruin to Miss Darcy's hopes? Could Elizabeth permit others to learn of her mother's insensibility and of her father's indifference? And what of Mary and Kitty and Lydia? With the entailment of Longbourn falling upon Mr. Collins, without proper husbands, her younger sisters and mother would suffer in poverty if either she or Jane did not marry well.

"Then it must be Jane," Elizabeth told her empty room as she crawled into bed. "A life with a renowned gamer will not permit me to be a cure for mama's nerves. My switch from Mr. Darcy to Mr. Wickham *shall* bring upon a case of the vapors, and I cannot bear what it will do to papa." Grief filled her throat, and Elizabeth permitted her tears free rein. "There will be no sleep this night or many to come."

Elizabeth's note arrived before nine of the clock. Darcy knew no sleep: His mind conjured up the scene of Elizabeth's following Mr. Wickham into Vauxhall's "private" walkway, and with each repeat performance Darcy imagined Mr. Wickham gathering Elizabeth into his arms to claim what should belong to Darcy.

Hers was the second message of the day. The first came from Mr. Wickham. Darcy noted the waif as the child messenger cautiously approached Darcy's door. Thinking the boy brought a message from Elizabeth, Darcy rushed through the halls to learn of the child's purpose. Mr. Thacker thought to send the boy away, but Darcy insisted the child be brought into the hall.

"A message, Sir." The boy's bottom lip trembled, but he held his ground, an admirable trait for one so small.

Darcy accepted the folded over pages.

"Are you to wait for my response? What were the lady's orders?"

"No lady, Guv. Jist a gent in a King's coat."

The child's words caused Darcy's apprehension to hitch higher.

"Wait here." To his butler, he said, "Mr. Thacker, I will require Murray's assistance, and keep the child close. Perhaps a bit of breakfast. Have you eaten, Boy?"

"No, Sir."

"Ask Cook to give the lad a proper welcome."

When Mr. Thacker disappeared into the bowels of Darcy House, the boy in tow, Darcy broke the seal upon the pages. He recognized the familiar script.

"As I suspected," Darcy murmured as he read Mr.

Wickham's demand for money in return for the letter.

"You sent for me, Sir?" His trusted footman appeared at his side.

"Yes. I require you to fetch my cousin, Colonel Fitzwilliam. Tell the colonel I require his service in regard to a missing letter."

Within an hour, a disheveled colonel escorted the boy to the place where the gentleman hired the lad.

"I will negotiate with Wickham," the colonel declared. "You are likely to kill him or give him what he wishes. I will do neither. However, Wickham may wish he was dead when I finish with him," Fitzwilliam added. "But I know how better to deal with a difficult popinjay than do you. Stay here. I will send word when I locate the scoundrel."

"Place the note on the table," Darcy told Mr. Sheffield when his valet carried the message to Darcy's quarters with news one of Gardiner's servants delivered it. "I will read it later."

"As you wish, Sir." Sheffield bowed from the room. Darcy's staff responded to the return of his dudgeon by tiptoeing through their duties.

"Your fault," he told the scene outside his bedroom window. "You sought perfection when none was to be had." Darcy closed his eyes to bring forth the image of Elizabeth as she was at the music shop: Her eyes upon him and what appeared to be the early stages of affection upon her features. With a sigh of resignation Darcy caught Elizabeth's note. "Might as well learn more of the depth of the lady's deceit. Another strike to my pride."

Ripping the wax seal away, Darcy unfolded the single page to read...

Mr. Darcy's Fault

> *I find I do not know how best to address the salutation of the letter. For many months, you were 'Mr. Darcy,' but of late, at least in my mind, you became 'William.' Yet, as this note is to serve as the end of our agreement, I suppose the more formal address is best.*

The air rushed from Darcy's lungs. He expected Elizabeth's withdrawal; however, the finality of her words left a gapping hole in Darcy's soul.

> *I decided to leave London so you should hold no fear of encountering me upon the street. My parting will prevent those awkward moments when we seek something of merit to say.*
> *In my leaving, I do beg one request, and I pray you will find it in you to act with honor. Mr. Bingley will marry Jane, and you must not turn aside Bingley's friendship because of his choice of wife. Rise above my decision and prove yourself the man of honor I came to know. Personally, I shall cheer Jane's news of her husband's most excellent friend, Mr. Darcy.*

Darcy often considered how he would go on with Bingley as his dearest friend if Elizabeth chose elsewhere. Now, he would learn firsthand if he were truly made of sterner matter.

> *Nightly, I shall pray for your health and happiness, but I shall not pray for your*

> *forgiveness. I do not deserve it because my conceit has brought enough doom to your door. I will close with my admittance of my most recent fault: I should have adhered to your warnings regarding Vauxhall; it is the most despicable of places.*
>
> EB

A postscript held the last blow to his heart.

> *The woman who claims the name of Mrs. Darcy will be blessed with the best husband to be found.*

Darcy collapsed upon the side of his bed. He did not know whether to rip the letter to pieces or to clasp it to his heart. He chose the latter as he lay across the counterpane. Perhaps he knew foolishness to think so, but Elizabeth wrote with affection. For a moment, Darcy permitted his hopes to wallow in their misery, but, at length, he forced reason to return.

"The lady may speak of the glory of being Mrs. Darcy, but Elizabeth Bennet prefers the moniker of *Mrs. Wickham.* So be it: She is no longer my concern. I will recover that foolish letter in order to protect Georgiana and Bingley. As for the Bennets, my wishes are they are sent to the devil."

With reluctance, Darcy made his way to his study. He stood by the window to look out upon the busy street.

"I will wait for Fitzwilliam's return, be done with this business, and then set a course for Derbyshire. I know my fill of the intrigues surrounding the lady. Good riddance, Elizabeth Bennet."

"I cannot imagine why Mr. Darcy did not call to escort you to services this morning," her aunt said in anxious tones.

"Perhaps he held additional family matters to which to attend." Jane glanced to Elizabeth in obvious caution. "Mr. Bingley says Mr. Darcy is most attentive to his family obligations."

Elizabeth steeled her response.

"The gentleman will not call today or ever again." She swallowed the panic rushing to her throat. "I thought it cruel to stretch out our understanding, which would end this week. I informed Mr. Darcy that we should not suit. I sent him a note early this morning to thank him for the honor of his proposal, but I refused him."

"Oh, Lizzy," Jane bemoaned. "I thought you learned to care for the man.'

Elizabeth kept her eyes averted to disguise the tears pooling in them.

"I require someone more spontaneous," she lied. "Mayhap someone such as Mr. Wickham."

"Did you not tell Mr. Wickham of your understanding with Mr. Darcy? Did I mistake Mr. Bingley's assurance of your sending Mr. Wickham packing?" Jane's eyes grew wide in disbelief.

"Such was my purpose in speaking to Mr. Wickham, but the more we conversed, the more I realized how much I always enjoyed Mr. Wickham's company." If she could convince Jane and Aunt Gardiner of her change of heart, others would follow suit.

Aunt Gardiner's attitude spoke of her suspicions.

"And what of Mr. Darcy's company? You would act the simpleton, Lizzy, if you allowed your fancy for Wickham to make you appear unpleasant in the eyes of a man ten times Wickham's consequence."

Elizabeth responded in her customary flippant tones, but her aunt's caution reminded Elizabeth of Charlotte's warning at the Netherfield Ball. Elizabeth erred then, and she held no doubt of the mistake she practiced now.

"Heaven forbid!" she declared, but a heavy hand squeezed her heart. "That would be a great misfortune indeed! Think how disagreeable it would be to recognize the finer qualities of a man one is determined to hate! Do not wish upon me such an evil."

"I apologize, Darcy," his cousin lamented. "I did not count on Wickham's wooing of the ale maid. The woman warned him of my presence in his room. He disappeared into the streets leading to the Thames."

"I am grateful you recovered the letter. I know you acted to save Georgiana, but I will offer my gratitude in the name of the Bennet family, my family, and Mr. Bingley's. Only through your diligence can Georgiana claim her place in Society."

The colonel sipped his brandy.

"You are being very hard upon yourself, Darcy." His cousin's eyebrow rose in curiosity. "I read the letter. Why did you not tell me Miss Elizabeth refused your initial proposal?"

"Pride. Conceit." Darcy shrugged his pain away. "Another of my many faults: I assumed I could make Miss Elizabeth happy, and so I exercised my will over hers."

"And now?"

Darcy closed his eyes to drive away the torment claiming his features.

"Miss Elizabeth sent a note earlier to end our agreement." He paused before adding, "This morning you did not ask why Mr. Wickham's note did not surprise me."

His cousin's expression spoke of the colonel's annoyance.

"Under the circumstances, you were quite calm: You did not put up a fuss when I demanded the privilege of confronting Wickham."

"That is because last evening after leaving Lockland Hall, I pursued Miss Elizabeth at Vauxhall, where she dined with her family and Bingley." Despite Darcy's best efforts, he shifted uneasily, so intense his cousin's regard. "I discovered my intended near the fireworks display. Needless to say, the lady had no idea I arrived: Miss Elizabeth was too busy following Mr. Wickham into the darkened pathways."

"I thought better of the lady," the colonel observed.

So did Darcy. His shoulders stiffened as if he prepared for an attack.

"Your recovery of the letter foiled the pair's plan to claim a portion of my fortune upon which to live. I am certain Miss Elizabeth regrets forwarding her refusal. If she waited one more day, the lady would know their plan failed. Who is to say? Perhaps Miss Elizabeth would have agreed to marry me simply to see her ambitions come to fruition. I suppose with Longbourn entailed upon Mr. Collins, Mrs. Bennet instructed her daughters to claim the highest prize."

"But even if Wickham knew success, five thousand pounds could not compare with your prospects," Fitzwilliam countered.

"Five thousand pounds would be enough to invest in Mr. Gardiner's and Mr. Bingley's many ventures. With Elizabeth's intelligence, she could lead Mr. Wickham into a life of respectability."

The colonel's expression grew bleak.

"Then I am pleased to grease their plans."

Darcy expelled a sharp, humorless laugh.

"Thanks to you, Mr. Wickham no longer holds anything I value. He will receive no ransom payment from me."

Chapter 10

ELIZABETH SLID THE NOTE under her sister's door before she made her way down the servants' stairs to exit through the kitchen. In the note, she explained her choice to Jane, not because she wished to claim the role of martyr, but because her heart would not permit Elizabeth to injure her father by providing him no explanation. Mr. Bennet reluctantly agreed to her marrying Mr. Darcy, and she knew her dear papa would hold many objections to Mr. Wickham's lack of a future.

"I thought you made other plans," Mr. Wickham declared when Elizabeth entered the alley leading to the mews. He caught the cloth bag she carried before taking her elbow. "My curricle is down here."

Elizabeth double stepped to keep up with his long strides.

"What is our destination?" she asked as Mr. Wickham hurried her along.

"Scotland," he announced as if Elizabeth should

know his response. Reaching the equipage, he tossed her bag behind the curricle's seat.

"To Scotland in a racing cart?" she said in disbelief.

Mr. Wickham caught her about the waist to lift Elizabeth onto the seat.

"I possess no fine traveling coach. As my wife, you will learn to make do."

Elizabeth wished to argue with him, but Mr. Wickham misplaced his amicable manners. Instead, she braced her seat so as not to tumble upon the road. It would take them several days to reach the Scottish border where marriage was as simple as speaking one's vows before a crowded room. When Elizabeth accepted Mr. Wickham's orders to meet him at midnight, she considered nothing but the misery of losing Mr. Darcy's regard. Would Mr. Wickham expect her to share quarters with him upon the road? And what of his service to the militia? Would Colonel Forester bother with reporting Wickham's desertion? Where would they live after speaking their vows? Would she ever see her dear family again? So many things she did not know. Elizabeth felt the fool for not clarifying Mr. Wickham's intentions before they set out together.

When the curricle lurched forward, Elizabeth caught harder at the bench.

"Did you speak to Mr. Darcy of your returning the letter?" she asked as the horse picked up the pace.

"I sent Darcy my demands," he hissed.

Elizabeth thought to ask for more details, but Mr. Wickham pulled up the collar of his jacket to ward off the night's chill, as well as her inquiries. She watched the London streets as they sped along, and she could not help but wonder which house held Mr. Darcy. Odd, but she had yet to view his home. *Now, you never will,* her wavering resolve reminded her. *Farewell, my dearest Darcy.* Elizabeth mouthed the words. She made her choice, and there was little she could do to alter it.

༄

"I must speak to Mr. Darcy now!" A rough voice brought Darcy awake. He fell asleep at his desk after imbibing in more brandy than was his custom.

"It is but six of the clock," his butler protested as Darcy staggered to the balustrade to view who dared disturb his household at such an ungodly hour.

"Gardiner?" Darcy looked down upon Elizabeth's uncle, and a buzz of dread shot down Darcy's spine. "What is amiss?" He started down the stairs, but Edward Gardiner rushed to meet him.

The man waved a note.

"I require your assistance," Gardiner declared. "Elizabeth is gone away with Mr. Wickham."

Darcy's steps slowed as a sharp pain returned to his gut.

"How does that concern me? Your niece terminated our agreement." With little success, Darcy attempted to keep the bitterness from his tone.

Gardiner thrust the note into Darcy's hands.

"Just read this. If you do not agree with the urgency of my request, I will leave you to your pride."

Darcy unfolded the two pages.

"It is addressed to Miss Bennet."

"Yes, last evening Jane took over the nursery duties so Mr. Gardiner could rest. One of the babes is cutting two teeth and is in misery. My niece did not return to her quarters until two of the clock. She found this letter upon opening her door. I searched the house and the mews, but to no avail. Jane says you hold a long-standing acquaintance with this man Wickham. I hoped you would know where I might search for the pair. Your compromising Elizabeth in order to see her to safety is forgivable, but not this madness. Lizzy means to sacrifice herself to protect her parents and her sisters. And what of this letter to which my niece eludes? Assist me, Darcy!"

"Permit me to read Miss Elizabeth's explanation," Darcy said in distraction.

> *Mr. Wickham means to have the ultimate revenge on Mr. Darcy, and without the letter's return, I hold no options.*

Darcy growled as he scanned the page for a clue as to her destination.

"I will run the bloody cur through!"

Ignoring Mr. Gardiner's agitation, Darcy barked out orders.

"Is my cousin in the guest quarters?'

"Aye, Sir."

"Wake him, and send to the mews for two horses!" He caught Gardiner's arm. "Come. I must change, and I need to read this with more care. Miss Elizabeth is not usually so obtuse. Do you suppose she possessed no idea of Mr. Wickham's plans?"

Gardiner followed Darcy to his quarters.

"Mrs. Gardiner claims Elizabeth played the role of carefree indifference throughout Sunday."

Darcy straightened his cravat but did not replace

it.

"She would. Anything of which I should be made aware?" He slid his arms into his jacket.

Gardiner appeared uncomfortable.

"Mr. Wickham joined Jane, Bingley, and Lizzy at Vauxhall two nights prior, but Jane swears Lizzy would not arrange an assignation. Apparently, Elizabeth told Mr. Wickham of your agreement."

Darcy paused his perusal of Elizabeth's letter.

"I came to Vauxhall to surprise Miss Elizabeth. I saw her with Mr. Wickham," Darcy confessed.

"Where?" Gardiner demanded.

"Entering the maze." Darcy closed his eyes to the damning image of Wickham and Elizabeth together. "Mr. Wickham caught her elbow. He led her into the darkness." Darcy admitted in bitterness, "I thought Miss Elizabeth followed him."

"Would Mr. Wickham force Lizzy into the maze?"

Darcy sighed in anguish.

"If Mr. Wickham threatened her family, Miss Elizabeth would follow him into the fires of Hell." Darcy scrubbed his face with his dry hands to drive away the exhaustion. "I am such a fool," he moaned.

"What of the letter this Wickham fellow holds over Lizzy's choices?"

"My cousin recovered the letter yesterday evening," Darcy confessed.

"Wickham is up to mischief. Does he know you have the letter?"

Darcy nodded curtly.

"But he must not have told Elizabeth; otherwise, no reason exists for her to cooperate with the dastard."

"Where could they have gone?" Gardiner lamented.

"Elizabeth speaks of marrying Mr. Wickham. That means they must travel to Scotland. If they did not elope, Mr. Wickham would need to keep Elizabeth hidden for a minimum of fifteen days, assuming he had the banns called yesterday. As Mr. Wickham serves with the militia stationed in Meryton and lately in Brighton, he would be required to have the banns announced in one of those parishes if he meant to seek a traditional wedding in the Church of England. Any other parish would require a fortnight's residence in addition to the calling of the banns. Wickham cannot hide Miss Elizabeth that long without your niece creating a bit of havoc. Their destination must be Scotland."

Gardiner agreed with Darcy in principle.

"Nevertheless, I will send Mr. Bennet a message to assure him of our efforts to recover Elizabeth and to confirm the local cleric did not call the banns yesterday in the Meryton church."

They changed horses twice before they earned news of a sighting of the pair. Darcy began to wonder if they erred in their choice of passages: The London Road led toward Durham and on into Scotland, but the colonel argued that Mr. Wickham would travel the familiar roads toward Derbyshire and Gretna Green.

"Ridin' in a fancy curricle," the groom at the Raven's Nest assured them. "The lady be little like you says and the gent tall."

"How long ago?" Darcy demanded as he tossed the groom an extra coin.

Mr. Darcy's Fault

"Mayhap two to three hours, but the gent's 'orse 'ad slowed to a walk."

"Had the man not changed horses?" the colonel asked.

"Not as I cud tell. Offered to let 'im a 'orse, but he'd refused."

Darcy could not resist asking. "Was the lady well?"

The groom shrugged.

"She be wrapped in her cloak, but she be shiverin'. Might be May, but the nights still 'old their chill."

The groom's words stabbed at Darcy's conscience. If he ignored Elizabeth's protests, as he should have, then she would not be in this position. At a minimum, he should have sent word he took possession of the letter. Even if they did not marry, Elizabeth deserved to know no one would learn of Darcy's folly. *My fault*, Darcy's conscience announced as he returned to the saddle. Only when he saw Elizabeth safe in her uncle's arms would Darcy forgive his pride for stealing away his reason.

"May we stop soon for a bit of tea?" Elizabeth asked through ice-cold lips. They traveled through a brief, but heavy, downpour, and she had yet to dry out.

"Have you a bit of coin?" Mr. Wickham asked with indifference.

Elizabeth kept her eyes on the horizon, in hopes the new day would bring the sun and warmth.

"A few pennies." In truth, Elizabeth sewed what money she saved over the last year into her clothes. She planned to purchase a vintage copy of her father's favorite Shakespearean play as a gift for his five and forty birthday, but as she prepared for her journey, Elizabeth took the extra precaution to hide what might prove to be her "escape" funds.

Her paternal grandfather always insisted that Mrs. Bennet include pockets upon her and Jane's dresses.

"The girls need a means to carry the pennies I give them."

Elizabeth sorely missed the scent of tobacco upon her grandfather's clothes and the sound of his voice as he read stories to her at bedtime. She regretted the fact her children would never know such memories. After her elopement, her farther would shut Elizabeth from his life.

"Enough for a cup of oats for the horse?" Mr. Wickham's question pulled Elizabeth from her misery.

She glanced to the animal, which knew as much exhaustion as did she. With the early streaks of daylight Elizabeth could note how the animal struggled.

"Most likely." She wondered why Mr. Wickham did not tend to the horse sooner. Were the coins he used for the tolls the last of his funds? Surely, if he approached Mr. Darcy regarding the letter, Mr. Wickham would have sufficient blunt to purchase them a proper meal and feed for his horse. Elizabeth thought to ask of the transaction between the gentlemen, but Mr. Wickham's countenance spoke of the dudgeon of his mind. *Did Mr. Darcy refuse to pay his former friend for the letter? If so, will my sacrifice be for naught? If scandal means to claim the Bennet name despite my efforts to divert it, I will not join with a man for whom I hold no respect.*

⁂

"They had a seven-hours' head start," Darcy grumbled as they took a late breakfast at a small inn. In his head, he calculated how many miles the pair could cover in the ten hours since their departure. He wished Gardiner called upon him as soon as Miss Bennet discovered Elizabeth's note. Perhaps if so, they would have caught Wickham's racing cart by now.

"I am certain they cannot be far ahead," the colonel declared.

"Will they remain on the toll roads?" Gardiner appeared as distressed as Darcy.

"Wickham cannot traverse many of the back roads while driving a curricle," Fitzwilliam assured. "He means to claim Miss Elizabeth to wife before anyone can overtake them. The toll roads are the best choice to expedite their journey."

The thought of Wickham taking liberties with Elizabeth set Darcy's blood boiling. They likely drove throughout the first night, but what of those nights to follow? Could he catch up with Elizabeth in time to prevent disaster?

"I will see to the horses," Darcy mumbled as he stood. What was a tasty bit of pork only a few minutes earlier turned hard to swallow.

Other than the occasional stop to permit the horse to drink its fill, they only broke their journey twice, both times at Elizabeth's insistence. Although she opened her cloak to the sun to permit her gown to dry, Elizabeth had yet to discover even a bit of warmth.

"Mr. Wickham," she murmured as she swayed upon the seat. If the gentleman did not catch her shoulder, Elizabeth would have toppled from the carriage. "I cannot go on," she pleaded.

Mr. Wickham brought the carriage to a halt.

"Is this a ploy to stall my intentions?" he demanded. He spoke to her seldom throughout the night and the day of their time together, but Wickham's tone announced his growing irritation.

Elizabeth clutched at her stomach before crawling down from the seat.

"No ploy," she gasped before retching in embarrassment.

Mr. Wickham eyed her in suspicion when she collapsed to her knees upon a grassy patch.

"You noticed the finger sign at the last crossroad," he accused. "You think because we are south of Lambton to reclaim Darcy's regard."

Tears filled Elizabeth's eyes at the thought of being in the same country as Mr. Darcy's childhood home.

"I had no knowledge of our being in Derbyshire," she argued. "My experience does not include traveling beyond London, and as to Mr. Darcy, I am well aware that door is closed." Despite the flurries her stomach had yet to abandon, Elizabeth struggled to her feet. "Why do you not speak to me of Mr. Darcy's letter? Has the gentleman possession of the letter?"

"Darcy remains a coward; he sent Colonel Fitzwilliam for the letter." Bitterness and something that sounded of remorse laced Mr. Wickham's tone. The news of Mr. Darcy's success brought Elizabeth comfort, and she breathed a bit easier.

"Then the colonel negotiated in his cousin's behalf?" she challenged. "Was Mr. Darcy generous?"

Mr. Wickham shot her a look of contempt. His snort of disapproval announced his acrimony did not recede.

"Fitzwilliam ransacked my quarters to recover Darcy's precious letter."

Mr. Wickham's revelation stole Elizabeth's breath away.

"Are you saying you received no compensation for the letter's return?" Her stomach rolled again, but Elizabeth did not think the chill invading her bones the cause of her upset. She braced her stance. "If so, why did you choose to claim me to wife?" Her mind raced. If Mr. Darcy had the letter, no reason existed for her to honor her agreement with Mr. Wickham.

A false smile graced Mr. Wickham's lips.

"Darcy will never wish you to know poverty. He will support me to protect you."

Elizabeth shook her head in denial.

"I will not permit you to use me to bring pain to Mr. Darcy."

"You will return to the carriage," Mr. Wickham growled.

"I will not."

Mr. Wickham jumped down to cross behind the curricle.

"I am not amused by this mutinous display."

Elizabeth backed from his reach.

"I cannot accompany you," she cautioned.

"You think Darcy will renew his attentions if I leave you upon his threshold."

Tears filled Elizabeth's eyes.

"No. Mr. Darcy would hold nothing but contempt for my participation in this ruse." Elizabeth eyed the tree line. Was there any means she could escape Mr. Wickham?

Mr. Wickham anticipated her thoughts for he

lunged for her. Elizabeth hiked her skirt to flee, but her half boots slid in a wet patch, and she pitched backward, slamming her head hard against the packed earth. Elizabeth blinked several times to clear her vision, but all she could see was the scowling countenance of Mr. Wickham before everything went black.

"He would not dare!"

Darcy ran his hand distractedly through his hair. It was dark when they entered his home shire, but his cousin convinced Darcy they could make better time if they stopped at Pemberley for the prime horse flesh found in Darcy's stable, rather than the sorry mounts they let at their last stop. At Pemberley's gatehouse, Mr. Ogram greeted them with the news Mr. Wickham called upon the manor earlier.

"I'd not permitted his entrance, but the lady be in a bad way. Mr. Wickham meant to beg for Mrs. Reynolds' assistance."

A cold shudder claimed Darcy's spine.

"How bad? Was the lady ill?" *Or had Mr. Wickham claimed intimacies, which injured Elizabeth?* The idea brought revulsion to Darcy's stomach.

"Not certain, Sir. She be slumped over Mr. Wickham's lap."

Darcy heard the colonel call his name, but he did not wait for his cousin's counsel. He kicked his horse's flanks hard: He must learn the truth of Elizabeth's ailments. *Please God*, he prayed as he kicked his mount a second time. *I cannot lose her now that Elizabeth is at Pemberley.*

At length, the manor came into view. The horse's hoofs clattered upon the bridge, and he pulled up on

Mr. Darcy's Fault

the reins. Sliding from the animal's back, he was on the ground and running toward the entrance before the colonel and Gardiner crossed the bridge.

Although it was near midnight, his butler jerked the door open just as Darcy reached it.

"Where is she?"

"The young lady?"

"Yes!" Darcy said with irritation. He wished to shake the answer from Mr. Nathan's lips.

"Up here, Mr. Darcy."

He looked to the third storey to find his housekeeper, Mrs. Reynolds, peering over the balustrade at him.

"Thank, Heavens!" Darcy sighed with relief. For a split second he thought Mr. Ogram erred or Darcy misheard. He mounted the stairs two and three at a time.

"How is she?" he pleaded. He fell in step beside the woman who served his family since he was but a babe.

"Doctor Stevens says the lady has a chill, which must be watched so it does not become a fever, and Miss Elizabeth struck her head when she fell."

Darcy stumbled to a halt.

"You know the lady's name?"

Mrs. Reynolds stared up at him in concern.

"Mr. Wickham explained the lady was your intended. I pray the rascal did not offer me another one of his Banbury tales. I would not have permitted him admittance to the manor if I thought he practiced one of his deceptions. I pray I did not err." She wrung her hands in agitation. "I could not wrap my head around the idea that you would permit Mr. Wickham to escort your lady to Pemberley, and the rogue did not provide me a logical explanation, but the lady corroborated Wickham's tale of your engagement."

A smile tugged at the corners of Darcy's lips: Elizabeth told Mrs. Reynolds they planned to marry.

"For once, Mr. Wickham spoke the truth. Miss Elizabeth and I are affianced." He caught Mrs. Reynolds' hand to give them a gentle squeeze. "I am pleased you took personal care of my lady." He motioned to her to lead on.

Mrs. Reynolds presented him a quick nod of agreement. Darcy had no care for whatever game Mr. Wickham exercised; Elizabeth's return to health claimed his concern. They stopped at one of the finer guest quarters.

"I believe your lady remains awake, but not for long," Mrs. Reynolds whispered.

Darcy closed his eyes to say a quick prayer before he reached for the door's latch.

"By the way, where is Mr. Wickham?"

"I assigned him quarters with the grooms this evening." Mrs. Reynolds said with indignation. "Even if he showed Miss Elizabeth a kindness I would not have Wickham under Pemberley's roof. Likely, he would be off with the silver before dawn."

Darcy stifled the laugh racing to his lips.

"The colonel and Miss Elizabeth's uncle will be here within moments. Would you see to their quarters?"

"Yes, Sir."

"And tell my cousin of Mr. Wickham's whereabouts. Colonel Fitzwilliam will take charge of the man."

Mrs. Reynolds remained at the door of Elizabeth's room only for a moment to provide the maid she assigned to Miss Elizabeth her instructions. Without asking, Darcy knew Mrs. Reynolds would insist the girl remain in the room as a chaperone. Darcy did not care who looked on: He only had eyes for the fragile figure resting upon the bed. From some five feet distance, he studied her sleepy-eyed countenance. The knot, which held his stomach prisoner since the day he departed the Gardiners' Town house, eased its grip.

"Miss Elizabeth," he whispered as he moved a chair closer to the bed.

Her eyes opened slowly, but the beginnings of a welcoming smile touched her lips.

"We must stop meeting this way, Mr. Darcy."

"As long as we keep meeting, Miss Elizabeth, I will know satisfaction."

Darcy sat beside the bed and caught her hand in his.

"As will I," Elizabeth murmured.

He kissed her knuckles.

"Thank Goodness, Mr. Wickham brought you to Pemberley."

"How come you to search for me?" Elizabeth slurred her words, and Darcy supposed Stevens gave her a bit of laudanum.

"Your Uncle Gardiner pleaded for my assistance once Miss Bennet discovered your note. You should have told me of Mr. Wickham's manipulations." Darcy traced circles upon the back of Elizabeth's hand.

"And you should have told me you recovered the letter," she countered, but Elizabeth intertwined their fingers.

"Your fault and my fault," he murmured. The tears

rushed to Darcy's eyes. He acted the fool, and Elizabeth paid the price for his prejudice. "Rest." Darcy brushed the hair from her cheek. "We will speak more on this tomorrow."

Her smile took on a wry twist.

"Shall I wake in the night's middle to find you overseeing my care?"

Darcy kissed her forehead.

"It is highly possible," he whispered. "After all, you are under my roof, and no one on my staff would dare to admonish the Master of Pemberley."

"Then, I shall anticipate the pleasure."

His cousin did not approve of Darcy's decision to pay Wickham's debts and to purchase a commission for the man.

"It is my wedding gift to Miss Elizabeth. She believes Mr. Wickham requires a bit of 'discipline' in his life."

Elizabeth did not wake during those long hours of that first night. Darcy knew that for certain for after seeing her uncle and Colonel Fitzwilliam settled and indulging in a warm bath, he sat in the chair to watch over her. Midday on Tuesday, he and Elizabeth held their first of many discussions on what occurred.

"The scoundrel requires an introduction to a flogging," the colonel grumbled, but Fitzwilliam agreed to make the necessary arrangements. "I know of a position in Newcastle," his cousin said with a wicked smile "Northumberland is uncomplicated. Mr. Wickham will have few opportunities to create havoc. Better so, it is over 150 miles removed from Pemberley."

Darcy smiled also.

"I will leave the choice to your discretion, Colonel."

On Wednesday, the colonel and Elizabeth's uncle departed for London with Mr. Wickham in tow. Darcy asked them to return for the wedding on the Monday after the third calling of the banns.

"No return to Hertfordshire?" Mr. Gardiner teased.

"I refuse to permit the lady further than Pemberley Park," Darcy declared in good humor.

After their families' departures, Darcy called upon Elizabeth in her quarters. The maid, Hannah, greeted him with a curtsy at Darcy knock on Elizabeth's door, but the girl remained in the room to guard Elizabeth's virtue.

"Are you prepared to view my home?" he asked as he assisted Elizabeth to her feet.

The smile on Elizabeth's lips said she too noted the irony of Hannah's staunch propriety when Darcy called upon her during the day. In truth, he spent several hours the previous two nights keeping Elizabeth company, while his household slept. Elizabeth nodded at the maid.

"Hannah tended to my appearance. Now, all I require is a handsome escort."

Darcy braced Elizabeth's first tentative steps. The color returned to her cheeks, but she remained quite weak. Stevens revised his initial diagnosis.

"Miss Elizabeth knew a chill, but I suspect she will recover quickly. The lady simply knew exhaustion."

Since returning to Pemberley, Darcy, too, caught up on missed sleep, and so he understood.

"At your service, Ma'am." Darcy nudged Elizabeth closer so he might support her weight if her feet failed her. "We will take it slow," he instructed.

"You have never failed me, Mr. Darcy," she said as they strolled though the passage toward the gallery.

Darcy leaned closer to prevent Hannah's hearing.

"I proved myself a failure on multiple occasions, but I am grateful for you forgiveness."

"We share enough blame," Elizabeth chastised. "No more regrets, Mr. Darcy."

Darcy swallowed his initial denial. Instead, he made small talk.

"How goes Hannah? If you are not pleased with her, I shall ask Mrs. Reynolds to replace her," he said privately.

Elizabeth glanced to where the girl, who was three years Elizabeth's senior, followed them at a respectable distance.

"Hannah knows little of being a lady's maid, but I like her. We will do well together." She smiled in that teasing manner Darcy adored. "I know even less of being the mistress of a grand estate. Perhaps you will wish to change your mind, Mr. Darcy."

Darcy knew better than to accept Elizabeth's challenge: The lady was well aware of his devotion to her. Instead, he began to describe the various portraits in the gallery, indicating his family's heritage, one of which he was very proud. Elizabeth listened attentively, asking the appropriate questions and commenting on the physical characteristics of his ancestors. At length, she paused to study a portrait of his five and twenty year old self. Darcy never liked the image; it made him uncomfortable to view himself as others might see him, but the look in Elizabeth's gaze had Darcy doing a double take.

"Is it a true likeness?"

Mr. Darcy's Fault

A brief lift of Elizabeth's lips told him she found his insecurity amusing.

"The portrait captures your consequence, Mr. Darcy, but not the man I have come to know."

"And which do you prefer?" he whispered.

"The former has his uses," she said in all seriousness, "but I most certainly prefer the latter."

Darcy sensed they were on the pinnacle of a new understanding, and he prayed Elizabeth would say the words he longed to hear. By silent consent, they spent the last two days speaking of everything except the need for their marriage. They both understood their intertwined paths and accepted their futures would be together, but Darcy wanted more from her.

"And these are your parents?"

Darcy looked affectionately upon the images of his father and mother.

"I was barely from leading strings when father commissioned this portrait. Father became angry when I would not sit still, which is the reason my mother placed a book before me."

"I shall keep Lady Anne's strategies in mind."

A wry twist of his lips said Darcy enjoyed her flirtations.

"You hold previous knowledge of my propensity for books, Miss Elizabeth."

Elizabeth squeezed his arm tighter.

"Yes. I am well aware of your many faults, Mr. Darcy," she declared in a familiar teasing tone. Darcy winked at her upturned face. "Do you suppose we shall make as striking a couple as did Mr. George Darcy and Lady Anne Fitzwilliam?"

Darcy's heart leapt with the possibilities.

"My father and mother were as darkness and sunlight–their complexions and features complete contrasts. We, on the other hand, will appear quite compatible." Darcy hesitated, but it needed to be said, so he ventured, "That is if our joining is your wish."

"You would still release me?" Elizabeth's eyebrow rose in challenge.

Darcy's shoulders stiffened.

"It would never be my wish, but I would prefer to claim a portion of your affections."

Elizabeth's eyebrow hitched higher.

"Hannah!" she called.

"Yes, Miss." The maid stepped from the shadows.

"Mr. Darcy and I must plead for your indulgence." Darcy glanced to the girl, who appeared as confused as he as to Elizabeth's manipulations. The maid half smiled and nodded her agreement. "Pemberley's master means to propose to me a second time, and I mean to accept." Darcy's breathing quickened. "Needless to say, it would not be appropriate for you to witness our private joy; therefore, I must ask you to turn about until I tell you otherwise."

A mischievous grin caught the maid's lips. The girl would have much to share below stairs.

"Yes, Miss."

When Hannah turned away, Elizabeth said, "Well, Mr. Darcy, I am waiting."

He caught Elizabeth's hand to bring the back of it to his lips.

"Miss Elizabeth Bennet, would you do me the greatest of honors by agreeing to be my wife."

A twinkle claimed in Elizabeth's expressive eyes.

"I believe I preferred the first proposal, at least the initial part of your avowals. Speak to me, Mr. Darcy, how ardently you admire and love me."

"Perhaps I should demonstrate my affections instead," Darcy groaned as he gathered Elizabeth to him to claim her lips in a kiss of passion. She shivered in his grasp. Struggling to recover his breathing, Darcy whispered, "I would hear your answer, Miss Elizabeth."

"Unlike you, I possess few examples of a companionable marriage," she offered in excuse.

"Yet?" Darcy implored.

Elizabeth laced her arms about his neck.

"Yet, I believe you when you tell me I will be more than an episode in your life."

"But can you share your affections with me?" he persisted.

Elizabeth smiled that special smile of all young lovers, and Darcy's heart melted.

"I must name one more fault to add to the litany I flung at your head on numerous occasions."

"And that is?" Darcy pressed.

She rose on tiptoes to brush her lips across his.

"It is your fault," Elizabeth whispered huskily, "that I fell most violently in love with you."

With a shout of joy, Darcy picked her up to spin Elizabeth in a circle. He kissed her again, this time with all the love in his heart.

"The lady said 'yes,'" he called to a blushing Hannah. "Pemberley will soon have a new mistress."

Hannah beamed at them.

"Pardon my saying so, Sir, but I would venture

you and Miss Elizabeth shall be the happiest couple in the world."

"Oh, yes," he and Elizabeth said in unison.

"It is settled between us already," Elizabeth declared. "I am the happiest of God's creatures. Perhaps other people said so before, but not one with such justice." She caught each of Darcy's hands and tugged him along behind her. "I am even happier than Jane," she announced boldly. "My sister only smiles. Look upon my blissful countenance: I laugh with open happiness."

Darcy caught Elizabeth to his side and led her toward the main staircase. They did not take note of the amusement crossing Hannah's expression nor did they hear her summation of this new development.

"I fear Mr. Darcy's very sedate world shall be turned upon its head. The master opened his life to a woman who will lead him on a merry dance, and we shall all serve as audience to the music."

Other Novels by Regina Jeffers

Jane Austen-Inspired Novels:
Darcy's Passions: Pride and Prejudice Retold Through His Eyes
Darcy's Temptation: A Pride and Prejudice Sequel
Captain Wentworth's Persuasion: Jane Austen's Classic Retold Through His Eyes
Vampire Darcy's Desire: A Pride and Prejudice Paranormal Adventure
The Phantom of Pemberley: A Pride and Prejudice Mystery
Christmas at Pemberley: A Pride and Prejudice Holiday Sequel
The Disappearance of Georgiana Darcy: A Pride and Prejudice Mystery
The Mysterious Death of Mr. Darcy: A Pride and Prejudice Mystery
"The Pemberley Ball" (a short story in *The Road to Pemberley* anthology)
Honor and Hope: A Contemporary Pride and Prejudice

Regency and Contemporary Romances:
The Scandal of Lady Eleanor – Book 1 of the Realm Series (aka *A Touch of Scandal*)
A Touch of Velvet – Book 2 of the Realm Series
A Touch of Cashémere – Book 3 of the Realm Series
A Touch of Grace – Book 4 of the Realm Series
A Touch of Mercy – Book 5 of the Realm Series
A Touch of Love – Book 6 of the Realm Series
A Touch of Honor – Book 7 of the Realm Series
His: Two Regency Novellas (includes "His American Heartsong," a Realm series novella, and "His Irish Eve," a sequel to *The Phantom of Pemberley*)
The First Wives' Club – Book 1 of the First Wives' Trilogy
Second Chances: The Courtship Wars

Coming Soon...

The Prosecution of Mr. Darcy's Cousin: A Pride and Prejudice Mystery
Angel Comes to the Devil's Keep
A Touch of Emeralds: The Conclusion of the Realm Series
The Earl Finds His Comfort
Elizabeth Bennet's Deception: A Pride and Prejudice Vagary

Meet the Author

Writing passionately comes easily to Regina Jeffers. A master teacher, for thirty-nine years, she passionately taught thousands of students English in the public schools of West Virginia, Ohio, and North Carolina. Yet, "teacher" does not define her as a person. Ask any of her students or her family, and they will tell you Regina is passionate about so many things: her son, her grandchildren, truth, children in need, our country's veterans, responsibility, the value of a good education, words, music, dance, the theatre, pro football, classic movies, the BBC, track and field, books, books, and more books. Holding multiple degrees, Jeffers often serves as a Language Arts or Media Literacy consultant to school districts and has served on several state and national educational commissions.

Regina's writing career began when a former student challenged her to do what she so "righteously" told her class should be accomplished in writing. On a whim, she self-published her first book Darcy's Passions. "I never thought anything would happen with it. Then one day, a publishing company contacted me. They watched the sales of the book on Amazon, and they offered to print it."

Since that time, Jeffers continues to write. "Writing is just my latest release of the creative side of my brain. I taught theatre, even participated in professional and community-based productions when I was younger. I trained dance teams, flag lines, majorettes, and field commanders. My dancers were both state and national champions. I simply require time each day to let the possibilities flow. When I write, I write as I used to choreograph routines for my dance teams; I write the scenes in my head as if they are a movie. Usually, it plays there for several days being tweaked and rewritten, but, eventually, I put it to paper.

From that point, things do not change much because I completed several mental rewrites."

Every Woman Dreams https://reginajeffers.wordpress.com

Website www.rjeffers.com

Austen Authors http://austenauthors.net

English Historical Fiction Authors http://englishhistoryauthors.blogspot.com

Chapter 1

Derbyshire, 1816

Darcy watched his family through the window of his study. Elizabeth and his children and his sons' nurses enjoyed a simple meal upon the side lawn. In reality, Elizabeth and young Samuel's nurse nibbled on the cakes and sandwiches while Bennet ran circles about the blanket spread upon the ground. Lily, the girl who provided the active care of Pemberley's heir, chased the boy, with laughter bubbling from both. Darcy could not remove the smile from his lips: His world knew perfection. He wished to join them, but how could the Master of Pemberley act with imprudence? Chasing butterflies and childish dreams on a late autumn afternoon…

As if she recognized how he longed to be one of their party, Elizabeth's head turned in his direction. A knowing smile graced her lips. If anyone had told him when he was but five and twenty that a headstrong sprite of a woman would bring him to his knees, Fitzwilliam Darcy would have scoffed in the man's face. Yet, his journey to Hertfordshire with his friend Bingley changed all that. At the outset, Darcy had accepted a variety of fanciful impediments to his and Elizabeth's connection, but that was before Elizabeth Bennet took him to task. Before she enumerated his abundant flaws rather than being quelled by his wealth and position. "How could I resist?" he murmured.

His wife raised her hand in greeting, and Darcy's heart lurched in response.

"God, if Mrs. Darcy held any idea of her power over me..." he acknowledged to the empty room. "Such an infatuating beauty."

Darcy knew he should return to his estate books, but he never tired of looking upon her. Even after more than four years of marriage, his eyes always sought the rich honey umber of her hazel ones, and he craved the feel of her skin beneath his fingertips: He carried a constant need to know his wife's ethereal excellence.

She stood to motion him to join her, but Darcy shook off the suggestion: He held responsibilities. Elizabeth's hands fisted at her waist, and a scowl crossed her beautiful countenance. The gesture reminded him of those early days of their acquaintance, and the same echo of desire that he first felt when he took her hand in his whispered in his ear. With a shrug of resignation, Darcy nodded his agreement.

Within seconds, he strode across the lawn to where Elizabeth waited. She smiled with his approach–a welcoming smile, the type to beguile a man from his reason.

"Papa!" Bennet called, scurrying toward him, arms lifted for Darcy's embrace.

He caught the boy in mid stride to lift the child above his head and to spin Bennet around.

"Gin, Papa!" Bennet squealed with delight.

Darcy spun his oldest a second time before he set the lad on the ground.

"Go to Lily," he instructed, and the boy scampered away to where Lily offered the boy a teacake, made without fruits or nuts, especially for his son.

Without asking Darcy's permission, Elizabeth deposited Samuel into Darcy's arms.

"Thank you for agreeing to join us," she whispered as he wrapped the blanket about Samuel's small body.

The boy, some two months of age, so resembled his mother that Darcy fell in love with the child instantly. They named the boy for his father's cousin, Samuel Darcy, a famous archaeologist, whose tragic death some four years prior had shaken Darcy's existence.

His heart clenched in caution. At moments such as these, Darcy's instinct told him to protect those he loved, for perfection was a fragile entity. Leaning into his shoulder, Elizabeth laced her fingers around his elbow.

"How could I deny your appealing gesture?" he teased in the manner of all lovers.

His gaze swept his wife's features: A bit of color kissed her cheeks, and her eyes sparkled with a sizzling depth of excitement. Her hair, simply styled, danced with auburn highlights, and she was the most beautiful woman of his acquaintance. A fierce tenderness filled Darcy's chest.

"Walk with me," he said as he leaned close.

Her gaze held his for several elongated moments, and Darcy imagined them alone–his whole world wrapped in his wife's capable hands. She smiled with intent.

"Bennet, stay with Lily and Mrs. Prulock. Your papa and I shall return in a few minutes. Then I will ask Mr. Mace to show you the new foal."

"Yes, Mama."

His son stood so proud it made Darcy's core claim a bit of arrogance. The boy reminded him of the child's revered grandfather, George Darcy.

He carried the sleeping babe cradled in the crook of his arm. Elizabeth sighed in contentment as they strolled across the groomed lawn.

"Is it not a beautiful day?"

"So beautiful," he murmured.

"Mr. Darcy," she protested, but he recognized the false disapproval in his wife's tone. "We were speaking of the weather."

"Lord save us from the English discussing the weather."

He smiled at her attempts to maintain a dignified expression.

Elizabeth displayed all the stubborn persistence she exhibited in Hertfordshire, but she conceded, "It is a hackneyed topic. Perhaps we should begin again."

Darcy paused before they entered the lower gardens.

"The beauty of which I spoke was the love of a woman worth knowing," he declared.

"I cannot believe you have not grown weary of our time together."

Darcy thought of the handful of occasions they had spent apart since their joining and frowned. It was odd, but since marrying Elizabeth Bennet, he had become quite content serving as Pemberley's master. He had been groomed for the role, but he never felt comfortable with his duty until he married the one woman who stirred his passions.

In Darcy's estimation, his wife was the missing part of the calculation–turning Pemberley from fine showplace to a home. Elizabeth had been more than his wife and the mother of his children: she was his lover, his confidant, and his best friend. She completed him.

"Trust me, my dear. For me, there is never enough

of you and the children."

A clearing of a masculine throat warned Darcy of his butler's presence; otherwise, Darcy would have indulged in an enticing kiss from his wife's all-too-tempting lips.

"Yes, Mr. Nathan."

"Pardon, Sir, but a necessitous post arrived by special messenger. I thought it best to seek you out. It is from Mrs. Fitzwilliam."

Darcy's frown lines met as apprehension skittered down his spine. It was not of Georgiana's nature to speak of exigency. He handed young Samuel to his mother before accepting the thick missive from the silver salver. Mr. Nathan bowed out when Darcy excused him with a flexing of his wrist and a mumbled

"Thank you," Darcy mumbled before flicking the sealing wax from the folded over pages.

"From Georgiana?" Elizabeth asked in concern. "Is something amiss with either your sister or our niece?"

She scooted closer to read bits over his forearm.

Darcy held a hand to signal her patience. He scanned the first page for details, but he could not immediately determine the urgency.

"Bear with me," he cautioned.

He knew his wife's deep affection for his sister. He read to determine the gist of Georgiana's letter. His sister was not one to raise alarm without true cause.

"My sister and baby Colleen are well."

He heard Elizabeth's sigh of relief, but he read on.

"Georgie is aggrieved of her husband's actions of late," he summarized. He flipped to the second page. "The unusual climate of this past growing season has levied a heavy toll on their reign at Yadkin Hall, and my cousin has taken the failures very ill."

Some two years prior, Darcy had returned from a

business journey to Northumberland to celebrate Christmastide at Pemberley, only to discover pure chaos under his roof, including uninvited guests and the news his sister had chosen their cousin, Colonel Edward Fitzwilliam, as her husband. Against Darcy's wishes, the couple had rushed their vows before the newly promoted major general returned to the war following Napoleon's escape from Elba.

Elizabeth shifted the child to her shoulder.

"I have worried from the beginning that Edward would not take well to the land."

Darcy scowled in disapproval.

"Both Matlock and I offered our assistance, but this year has challenged even the most creative estate master. My cousin has never spoken a syllable of his struggles," he said as he returned to the tightly spaced pages. "My God! Has Bedlam claimed Edward's good sense?"

"Tell me quick," his wife insisted.

If he could place his hands upon his cousin's neck, Darcy would have taken prodigious delight in throttling Edward Fitzwilliam.

"The major general left early on Wednesday last, saying he meant to examine the tenant farms. When he did not return for supper, Georgiana sent out men. For three days, my sister has searched for Edward, but with no word of him. On Friday, Georgie received a simple, one-page note, saying the major general traveled to London and did not know when he would return to Oxfordshire."

"Poor Georgiana," Elizabeth sympathized. "She must be quite beside herself with worry. Your cousin has acted in a most unexpected manner."

Darcy's eyes remained on the pages he held.

"I may kill him," he grumbled.

"When do we depart for Whitney?"

He glanced at his pocket watch. It did not surprise him that his wife meant to rush to Georgiana's side; he and Elizabeth were of the same mind in such matters.

"It is eleven of the clock," he thought aloud. "Is it worth the bother to depart today? The earliest we might leave would be one. I will not permit you to travel by night: The roads are too dangerous."

"At least you did not consider leaving me at Pemberley."

Darcy shook his head in denial.

"I could travel quicker alone, but I am likely to be absent from Derbyshire for some time. I cannot tolerate being from you and the children so long. Moreover, Georgiana will require your good sense in how best to respond to the major general's unprecedented actions."

"Then we should…"

Darcy's exclamation interrupted his wife's planning.

"We *cannot* leave! We have Samuel's christening after Sunday's services. Everything is arranged."

"We shall simply reschedule the event. I will dash off a note to Jane and Mr. Bingley, explaining the necessity of postponement. Samuel will forgive our delay. Will *you* not, my love?"

She traced a finger along the boy's chin, and his son sucked on the tip of it.

"Are you certain?" Darcy asked. "I know you have gone to great measures for the celebration."

"It is nothing which cannot wait until this situation with Georgiana is resolved."

"You are a magnificently kind hearted woman, and I am so grateful that you have blessed me with your favor."

He kissed her forehead and held the moment as he breathed in his wife's essence. Only her presence provided him any peace.

"Then shall we set a time of one for our departure?"

Elizabeth caressed Samuel's fluff of hair.

"We will only manage five hours of travel today, but that is still five hours closer to Mrs. Fitzwilliam."

Darcy refolded the letter and placed it in an inside pocket.

"You set the servants to preparing our trunks, and I will speak to Mr. Mace about the carriages."

Elizabeth went on tiptoes to kiss his cheek.

"Georgiana is a reasonable woman. She knew when she sent the letter we would be on the road post haste. Our sister will not act from unnatural consequences."

"I know you speak the truth, but worry has always been my shroud where Georgiana is concerned."

They rolled from Pemberley's doorstep at a quarter past one. Two carriages, the one in which he, Elizabeth, and Bennet rode, and the other containing Hannah, Elizabeth's lady's maid, Mr. Sheffield, Darcy's valet, Lily, Mrs. Prulock, and Samuel. Elizabeth had permitted Bennet to ride with them to pacify the child for not visiting with the newest horse in the Darcy stable.

"You must mind your Papa," Elizabeth warned the boy when Murray lifted the child to the coach.

"Yes, Mama," he said with importance.

Darcy knew Elizabeth considered their eldest of his nature, but he recognized how the child held as much of her mulish impetuousness as Bennet did the mannerisms of the Darcys.

Darcy placed the boy beside him on the rear-facing seat. From the earliest days of their marriage, he had taken his family with him when business necessitated his travel. Although little more than two years of age, Bennet had shown himself quite intelligent, and Darcy relished instructing his child in the ways of travel and the land's geography.

"A gentleman always permits the lady to sit as such," he explained.

Bennet nodded with enthusiasm.

"Mama says some come ill, but not Mama."

Darcy chuckled.

"No, not your Mama. She is made of a sterner nature."

"'Terner,' the boy repeated with an approving grin. "I be 'terner too, Papa."

Darcy ruffled the child's hair.

"I could ask for nothing more from my eldest."

Elizabeth smiled at their son.

"We will stay with Aunt Georgiana. You will visit with baby Colleen. I expect you to assist Lily and Mrs. Prulock with Samuel and Colleen. As you are Papa's heir apparent, it is important for you to be kind to the babies."

The boy frowned.

"Kin I p'ay also, Mama? Wily p'ays good games."

Darcy watched as Elizabeth swallowed her mirth.

"Certainly, my darling. Your Papa and I both believe little boys should learn their responsibilities, but they should also have time each day to enjoy play."

It took over eight and fifty hours for his party to reach Yadkin Hall. If he had not been so selfish about keeping his family close, Darcy could have eased his sister's anguish some twelve hours earlier, but then his own torment would have taken precedence.

He had come to accept his dependence on Elizabeth and his children for his concord. He often prayed that when he and Elizabeth reached the end of their lives,

God, in His wisdom, would take him first. Now he had found her, Darcy did not believe he could live one day without Elizabeth by his side.

At length, his carriage rolled into the circle before Yadkin Hall. It was a modest estate–simple in comparison to Pemberley or Matley Manor, but the house was in good repair. It reminded Darcy of a cross between Netherfield Park and Longbourn. The manor's main door swung wide, and his sister stepped into the early evening light, the major general's butler flanking her, a lantern held high.

Darcy watched Georgiana's lips move, speaking his name. It had been the way with them. After their father's death, he had become not only Georgiana's brother, but also her guardian.

"Go to her," Elizabeth whispered as she adjusted the sleeping Samuel in her arms. "Murray will see to our needs."

Darcy caressed her cheek, and without another word to his wife or a command to his waiting servant, he released the door's latch and set down the steps. Bounding from his coach, he rushed to his sister's side, catching Georgiana in his embrace. She buried her face in his chest to hide her sobs.

How many times had he held her as such? From more falls and scrapes than Darcy cared to recall and from that fateful day when Georgiana thought her heart broken by George Wickham, but nothing of this nature. He always thought Edward Fitzwilliam the most honorable of men, but his cousin's actions befuddled all reason.

The major general had abandoned his wife and child: An act beyond Darcy's forgiveness. Displeasure, of no common degree, claimed his reason.

"Come now," he whispered to Georgiana.

He slipped his handkerchief into her hand.

"We will settle this inside. First, you should greet Elizabeth and your nephews."

He heard Georgiana swallow hard and recognized her efforts to stifle her tears. After a long pause, his sister raised her chin.

"Certainly," she said in a rasp and stepped from his embrace.

Majestically turning her head, his sister donned her most welcoming smile.

"Elizabeth," she called. "And Samuel," Georgiana cooed. "I have missed you both." Georgiana caressed the child's dark auburn hair. "He has the look of you, Elizabeth."

"So says your brother," Elizabeth acknowledged as she brushed a kiss across Georgiana's cheek.

"Wantie!"

The group looked up to see Bennet rushing toward Georgiana.

Georgiana caught the boy and lifted him to her.

"My goodness!" Georgiana laughed as she kissed Bennet's cheek. "You have grown so tall in my absence. And so handsome."

"I am to a'sist nurse with 'Amuel," Bennet declared.

Georgiana nuzzled the boy's cheek.

"You must do the same with Colleen. Your cousin will depend upon your protection as I have always depended upon your papa."

Bennet's arms went about Georgiana's neck.

"Tect you and Mama too."

"Then we are blessed," Georgiana assured.

Less than an hour later, Darcy, Elizabeth, and his sister gathered in Georgiana's sitting room.

"Now, explain what has occurred to drive the major general from his home."

Georgiana squirmed as she always had when he confronted her, but his sister did not look away: She was maturing.

"When we first arrived at Yadkin Hall, life appeared idyllic. The days were long, but hope reigned. My husband met with his tenants and planned for a future, while I oversaw the manor. But, as you well know, the weather has not been kind to those who depend upon the land. It speaks well of Edward that my husband does not shirk his responsibility, but the major general has permitted his failure to…"

Georgiana caught her handkerchief to dab her eyes.

Elizabeth cautioned.

"A man who has known so much success in the military would naturally take any strife as a personal defeat."

Georgiana presented them a weak smile.

"I understand my husband's need for accomplishments…"

"I do not!" Darcy insisted. "I will never understand a man who deserts his wife and children."

Elizabeth softened his words.

"You were groomed to know the land; whereas, as a second son, Edward excels at stratagems and political history."

Darcy wished to remind his wife that he was well recognized for his love of history and for his financial maneuverings, but he swallowed his words. This was not a time to permit his pride center stage.

"What precipitated the major general's withdrawal?"

Georgiana's forehead scrunched up in confusion.

"In truth, I hold no definite cause. The evening before Edward's disappearance, my husband worked late in his study, only briefly appearing in the nursery when I visited with Colleen. Although the estate books are never a pleasure that Edward would claim, he did not appear worried by his accounting. I did not see him after that brief encounter in the nursery. When I awoke the following morning, Mr. Stacey brought word the major general meant to call upon several of the tenants and would return for the mid day meal. As I explained in my letter, when Edward did not return by nightfall, I sent out search parties."

Darcy studied Georgiana's countenance. His sister withheld some pertinent facts, but he would wait for a more opportune moment to discover the complete truth. He prayed Edward had not raised his hand to Georgiana. If so, Darcy would be forced to call his cousin out.

"Is the major general at Lockland Hall? You said Edward's message came from *London*."

"No." Georgiana's shoulders stiffened. "I thought my husband would either call in at his family's Town house or at Darcy House, but both households remain closed according to the messenger I sent to carry my concerns to the major general. Boyd returned without finding my husband. I possess no knowledge of Edward's whereabouts."

Darcy scowled.

"And you have received only the one message?"

Georgiana fished into a pocket in the apron she donned while tending the babies. She withdrew a crumpled paper and handed it to Darcy. Grudgingly, he unfolded it to read:

> *My dearest Georgie,*
> *It grieves me to know I have failed you and Colleen, but it is best you return to Darcy's care. Your brother is built to protect you from*

harm, whereas I am built for war. I will speak to my former commander. Perhaps I can purchase another commission. When my plans are complete, I will send word. Please forgive me...
              Your loving husband, E.F.

Darcy bit back the curse, which sprang to mind.

"It appears I am to London tomorrow," he said through tight lips.

"How shall you know where to begin your search?" Georgiana asked. "Should we not permit my husband his way? I would not wish to force Edward to return to a situation he finds intolerable. Could we not tell everyone the major general answered the call of service? I would be pleased to return to Pemberley with you and Elizabeth."

A slight shake of Elizabeth's head warned Darcy not to accept Georgiana's wish to avoid a confrontation with her husband.

"Although I would be delighted to have you and Colleen at Pemberley, I owe my cousin an obligation. Edward holds two familial connections, and we must set his estate aright for the sake of the Fitzwilliam name," he said as if nothing untoward had happened.

Georgiana's lips moved, but no sound escaped.

"What if..." she whispered.

"You will always have a home with your brother," Elizabeth assured. "But first we must determine Cousin Edward's whereabouts. You would not wish to turn from the major general if he is suffering."

"Certainly not," Georgiana affirmed. "I desire only peace for my husband."

Darcy suspected the word "peace" held a clue to the root of what had occurred under Yadkin Hall's roof, but he held his tongue. He had learned long ago to watch and listen before acting.

"There are too many questions without answers. We must begin with whether Edward is in dire straits. From there, all other decisions will become evident."

Georgiana nodded her understanding.

"I shall send word to Mr. Stacey for your coach's preparations for eight of the clock, unless you would prefer to leave earlier."

"Eight is adequate," Darcy assured.

His sister's mood frightened him. He had not observed her so despondent since that fiasco with George Wickham, but after her marriage to their cousin, Georgiana had seemed to put her earlier self chastisement behind her, and in Scotland, she confronted Wickham upon the Ayrshire moors.

Now, she wished to retreat to Pemberley. Despite his natural desire to protect her, Darcy realized the truth of Elizabeth's caution: If Georgiana returned to Pemberley–if his sister abandoned her marriage, she would never leave Derbyshire again. Georgiana would rot away under his roof, never to sparkle again with happiness.

Georgiana made her excuses to tend to Darcy's wishes, and once her footsteps receded, Elizabeth suggested, "Perhaps you should seek the assistance of Thomas Cowan. The man likely knows more of the major generals' favorite stomping grounds than you."

"Yours is an excellent suggestion," Darcy said. "Now, provide me your opinion as to what has occurred between Georgiana and the major general."

"When we were all in Scotland, I cautioned Georgiana that just because Edward pronounced his vows did not mean the major general could leave behind the decade of devastation to which he stood witness, but it appears she ignored my advice."

"And the major general also," Darcy agreed. "Before we recovered Georgiana from that reiver's cottage, my cousin was near mad with grief at the possibility of losing his wife. How could a man consumed by a woman not ten months prior walk away from her as if she meant nothing to him?"

"I recall your expressing concerns regarding your cousin's transition to civilian life," Elizabeth mused.

"Yes, but Edward promised me Georgiana would never know pain by his hand. He pronounced my sister his world. The major general swore when he returned to Pemberley to discover the woman Georgiana had become he felt as if God meant for him to leave his position and to claim the love of a wife and family...to know the meaning of *home*. It is all very vexatious."

Irritation crossed Elizabeth's features.

"Yet, the major general did not execute the one response that would assure his happiness: He did not trust Georgiana with his confidences. The situation with the lost crops is not the issue. Georgiana's dowry, as well as Edward's position as an earl's son, would protect the estate and the land until better times arrive. I warned the major general he must share with Georgiana the part of him he withheld from all others–to trust his wife with what haunted him.

"I told your cousin that only when he had acted as such would he know contentment. Since the death of your father, you and your cousin have served as Georgiana's guardians, and Edward has clung to that mantle. He has never permitted Georgiana to be the protector of his heart. Your cousin has kept his wife as his *subject* rather than as his companion. Even if you convince the major general to return..."

"You are saying that if my cousin refuses to alter the manner in which he approaches his marriage, I should encourage him to relinquish my sister to my care?"

Anger swelled Darcy's heart: Anger with Edward

for not recognizing his shortcomings, anger with Georgiana for rushing into marriage, and anger with himself for not protecting his family. How could Darcy drive his cousin from his life in order to safeguard his sister?

Elizabeth answered in disappointed tones.

"I am saying there is no easy way to go. Either your cousin or Georgiana will know a broken heart."

CPSIA information can be obtained at www.ICGtesting.com
Printed in the USA
LVOW04s1458210515

439401LV00007B/299/P